AFRICAN ADVENTURE

Amateur sleuth Eve Masters has just married the man of her dreams, David Baker, on the romantic island of Crete. Now they are heading off on their honeymoon to Tanzania. Eve has promised her new husband not to get involved in any more mysteries — but when one of their safari party is murdered, she can't help but get drawn in. It isn't long before she's in the middle of a very dangerous game . . .

IRENA NIESLONY

AFRICAN ADVENTURE

Complete and Unabridged

LINFORD
Leicester

First published in Great Britain in 2017

First Linford Edition
published 2019

A catalogue record for this book is available
from the British Library.

ISBN 978–1–4448–4035–3

Published by
F. A. Thorpe (Publishing)
Anstey, Leicestershire

Set by Words & Graphics Ltd.
Anstey, Leicestershire
Printed and bound in Great Britain by
T. J. International Ltd., Padstow, Cornwall

This book is printed on acid-free paper

1

Eve Masters stared at the man pointing a gun at her. How could this be happening yet again? She hadn't interfered this time — well, not so that anyone would notice, or so she told herself.

Eve had a habit of ending up in situations such as this, but she had convinced herself that she would try to avoid trouble. She didn't want to put her new husband through any more trauma, even though she craved excitement.

The man walked towards her and Eve started to tremble. Was this it? Would her life end now, so soon after marrying the man of her dreams?

However, her captor merely pushed her roughly into a chair.

'You can stay there,' he growled. 'The boss hasn't yet decided what he wants to do with you.'

The man left, slamming the door behind him. Eve heard the key turn and felt tears welling up.

A memory of her wedding day flashed through her mind. It had been amazing getting married on a beach on the island of Crete, where they lived. All she wanted now was to be with David.

Eve wondered what her new husband was thinking. He must have discovered that she was missing, but what would his reaction be?

Surely he wouldn't imagine that she had left him? She had given no indication that she was unhappy or had made a mistake; quite the opposite in fact. She hoped that he had informed the police that he couldn't find her, but would they do anything? Would they say that she hadn't been gone for long enough for them to take any action?

Then an awful thought struck her. It could be virtually impossible for the police to find her. Eve herself had no idea where she was. She had passed out when she was hit on the head at the hotel, and for all she knew the man could have driven her to a shack in the middle of nowhere. There might be wild animals outside. How she wished that she was in David's protective arms.

Then she shivered; perhaps she wouldn't ever be held by her husband again . . .

★   ★   ★

Only a week ago David Baker and Eve Masters had begun their honeymoon in Kenya and Tanzania. It had started off particularly well, so how could everything have gone so wrong?

Even the lengthy plane journey to Kenya had been enjoyable. They had watched an entertaining film and enjoyed delicious food. Eve had tucked into a mushroom and truffle filo tart, while David enjoyed a beef Wellington. Both followed their main courses with a rich chocolate mousse.

'More champagne, sir, madam?' the

flight attendant asked.

'Oh yes, please,' Eve replied immediately.

She loved champagne, and it was one of the many advantages of flying first class.

'I'll have another glass as well, thank you,' David added.

Eve was surprised. David didn't usually drink much as he liked to keep his head clear for writing. He was an author, but he was on holiday now — so why not indulge a little?

'Only another couple of hours and we'll be landing in Kenya,' he said, clinking her glass. 'I'm getting quite excited. Are you?'

'I can't wait to get there. I've been looking forward to this holiday for such a long time. I only hope that you will love Africa as much as I do.'

'I'm sure I will, darling. You've made it sound wonderful.'

David and Eve had got married a week before their honeymoon, but they'd had friends staying, so had delayed their trip. They were flying to Mombasa and would spend one night at a game reserve in Kenya before travelling into Tanzania for a two-week safari, followed by another week relaxing in a hotel in Mombasa.

David was hoping the honeymoon would make Eve forget about the turmoil surrounding their wedding. Since moving to Crete three years previously, Eve had found herself involved in all kinds of murder and mayhem, just escaping with her life on many occasions.

She'd promised David she wouldn't get involved in anything dangerous again, but could she keep her promise? It worried David sick when Eve went out of her way to catch criminals. He hoped she'd had her fill of excitement to last a lifetime.

Although Eve had been frightened when she was kidnapped on Crete days after their wedding, the fear had worn off and she was already beginning to view the whole escapade as exciting.

'I must go and do something with my make-up,' she suddenly said. 'I'm sure I look a fright.'

'You look beautiful, darling; as always.'

Eve kissed David before getting up. He leaned back in his comfortable seat and sighed with relief. Much as he loved Crete, he was glad they were getting away. It had been a traumatic couple of weeks with Eve trying to solve another crime, when she should have been focusing on their wedding. However, against all the odds, the celebrations had gone off swimmingly.

A few minutes later, Eve retuned to her seat, looking perfect. She always took great care of her hair and make-up, and even after this long plane flight, she had managed to stay looking good.

Eve was a very attractive woman with shoulder length blonde hair, green eyes and a slim figure. She was in her mid-forties, but looked younger. David was also handsome, with sleek black hair and piercing blue eyes. Together they made a stunning couple and were capable of turning heads when they walked into a room.

They held hands as the plane carried them towards Mombasa, sitting in comfortable silence.

★   ★   ★

David and Eve looked around the hectic arrivals lounge. People were dashing everywhere. Still, it didn't take them too long to find the man holding up their holiday company's name.

A couple in their sixties was standing there already. As soon as Eve had given their names to the tour guide, the woman started speaking.

'Hello! We're Joan and Ken Ferguson. We're so excited about this holiday. We've been waiting until Ken's retirement to take it. Now, at last, we're here.'

'We're Eve and David,' Eve replied. 'We're here on our honeymoon.'

'Oh!' Joan said brightly. 'Second marriages for both of you, I expect?'

This comment made Eve bristle. How dare Joan suggest that they were old? She was reminded of Betty back on Crete, who never minced her words when it came to Eve. They had had many a battle over the last few years.

'This is my first marriage.' Eve spoke sharply. 'I have had a very successful career, so haven't had the time to devote myself to anyone else. A marriage takes commitment and I wouldn't have wanted to get married if I couldn't give it my all.'

With that, she turned and kissed David full on the lips, hoping to embarrass Joan. She imagined Joan would think her rude, but she didn't care. She had come on this holiday to be with David, not to make new friends.

However, a rather glamorous couple in their mid-thirties then turned up, and Eve immediately introduced her-self, thinking that these two were more her sort of people.

'Richard and Sophie Blair,' the man said.

'These two are on their honeymoon,' Joan piped up.

Eve glared at Joan, who didn't seem to notice. Eve could speak for herself. She didn't need the likes of Joan Ferguson to talk about her.

'How lovely,' Sophie said. 'We've only been married a year ourselves. Have you any wedding photos with you? I would love to see them.'

'Of course I have. They're all saved on my laptop. I'll show you them one day during the trip.'

Sophie smiled, and Eve thought that it might not be so difficult to make friends on this holiday.

Before long everyone else had arrived. There was one other couple, Kate and James Thompson, who looked to be in their fifties; two single women, Karen Lane and Joyce Palmer; and a man on his own, Lawrence Brady.

The guide led them onto the coach.

'Good morning. My name is Gary and I'll be your guide during the safari. I'm an ex-pat and I've lived in Kenya for the past twenty years. Your driver is Adhama. He knows where all the best spots are for viewing wildlife.'

Eve smiled. She loved wild animals, and couldn't wait to get out into the bush.

The coach started the journey towards Taita Hills, a game reserve in the south east of Kenya. It was about a three-hour drive, during which time many people nodded off. The flight had been a long one, but Eve and David had managed to get some sleep in their comfortable first class seats.

Eve surveyed her fellow travellers with interest, particularly the ones on their own. Karen looked to be in her twenties, and Eve thought she was quite pretty, with long, dark brown curls and dimples in her cheeks.

Lawrence had sat next to her and seemed to have engaged her in conversation. Every now and then, Eve heard Karen laugh and wondered if there might be a holiday romance there.

Joyce Palmer looked to be in her early seventies. She sat in front of Eve and David and occasionally turned round to chat. Eve found her interesting, as she seemed as well travelled as she was.

Finally, Eve did drop off to sleep, her head on David's shoulder. The coach trundled along towards the game reserve.

2

It was four in the afternoon and everybody had boarded the Jeeps. There were two for this game drive, although there would be a larger vehicle in Tanzania, which would take all of them.

Eve was pleased to see that Sophie and Richard were in their Jeep, but not so happy that Joan and Ken had got in as well. The more she listened to Joan, the more annoyed she got. Her similarity to Betty back home was quite unnerving.

Eve was being a little unfair as she didn't really know Joan, but she had a habit of judging people very quickly without giving them a chance.

Both Joan and Ken were kitted out in safari shorts and shirts. *Typical tourists*, Eve thought. She had her own style, and was wearing fitted navy shorts with a white T-shirt, which showed off her perfect figure and tan to full advantage.

Both Jeeps headed off towards the bush. Joan shouted out quite soon after they had left.

'Look! There's a couple of giraffes. Where's my camera?'

Eve cringed. Really, that woman talked so loudly that she would probably scare away the animals. Still, Eve was pleased to see the first of the wildlife this trip, and she already had her camera poised and ready to take photos.

Not long afterwards, everyone was thrilled to see a pride of lions, especially as there were several cubs.

'Wow,' David said. 'You're right, Eve — this is fascinating. I didn't imagine that it would be so amazing being this close to the animals.'

Eve squeezed David's hand, both pleased and relieved that he was enjoying himself. After all, the honeymoon destination had been her choice.

'I could just get out and cuddle the

babies,' Joan piped up.

'Well, that would be a bit silly, wouldn't it?' Eve said to her, receiving a glare in response.

Eve was looking forward to getting to Tanzania when they would all be in the same Jeep and Joan's voice might be drowned out by the others.

All of a sudden, Gary whispered, 'Look — there's a cheetah underneath that tree.'

Eve gasped. Cheetahs were her favourite big cats and she hadn't seen that many on her previous trips to Africa. She was delighted to see one on her first game drive of this holiday.

'It's amazing, Eve,' David said. 'I'm repeating myself, but I can't help it. It's just so exciting.'

Eve nodded, taking photos.

Sophie turned round to speak to Eve and David.

'I didn't think I would get excited at seeing animals in the wild, but I am. However, they are just a little too close for comfort.'

Eve smiled.

'It's amazing, isn't it? Mind you, I do think we'll be safe enough in the Jeep, Sophie.'

Sophie nodded, but moved closer to Richard as if she needed protection.

The game drive continued for another hour, satisfying everybody with sightings of zebra, impala and wart hogs, as well as more lions.

* * *

Eve had heard other people at the lodge talking about going on a night game drive, and wondered why Gary hadn't told them about this opportunity. She decided to go and find him. She didn't want to miss out on this. It sounded particularly exciting.

She thought she'd go and see if Gary was in his room. After all, he had told them to just come and knock at his door if they had any problems. As she approached, she saw the door ajar. She was about to knock when she heard voices. Eve, being Eve, couldn't help but stop and listen.

'If he can't be trusted, he'll have to be got rid of,' she heard Gary say.

'That's a bit extreme, isn't it, boss?' the other man said.

The other person had an African accent, so she presumed that he was a local.

'Needs must, Hamisi,' Gary said. 'If any of you refuse to follow orders, you can be replaced.'

Eve gasped. What on earth was going on here? Did Gary mean to kill someone, or was he simply talking about sacking an employee? She didn't know what to do. Should she leave before getting embroiled in another mystery?

However, this sounded intriguing and she immediately forgot about her promise to David to keep her nose out of the affairs of others.

Then again, she did want to go on the night game drive — so she had no choice but to speak to Gary. Eve steeled herself and knocked.

'Come in,' Gary shouted.

He seemed a little irate. Eve decided it was best to ignore his tone. After all, he could be a killer.

'Hello,' she said. 'I'm sorry to disturb you, but I heard something about a night game drive?'

'I'm so sorry,' Gary said, now putting on his best smile. 'It's very remiss of me. I can arrange for you and your husband to go on one this evening at seven o'clock, if that suits.'

'That will be great,' Eve replied. 'Thank you.'

She left, her mind in turmoil. What on earth was that all about? She had glanced at the other man, but he had avoided eye contact.

Should she tell David what she had overheard? Probably better not to. He'd think that she was interfering again, plus she didn't think that she would be able to hide her excitement if she did tell him. No, she'd be wise not to say anything.

However, as she wandered towards her room, her thoughts were confused. Perhaps it would be better to forget the conversation. She had promised David she wouldn't get involved in any more crimes, and she knew she should keep this promise. On the other hand, she was intrigued. Who on earth did Gary want to get rid of and why?

* * *

Eve and David left their room just before seven. They were both looking forward to the night game drive, although Eve hadn't been able to get Gary out of her mind. She hoped David hadn't noticed that she was distracted. She had tried hard to be attentive towards him, but he was no fool.

Entering the lobby, Eve was relieved that Joan and Ken weren't there. However, Kate and James Thompson stood waiting, as did Karen, who came up to Eve, smiling.

'I'm so excited about going into the

bush in the dark,' she exclaimed.

'Me too,' Eve replied. 'It will certainly be an experience.'

'Don't you think our tour guide is handsome? He looks so fit. I have to admit that I'm smitten.'

Eve wondered why Karen was confiding in her. They barely knew each other! Then she thought of what she had heard Gary say earlier. He was not a man to be trusted — but there was no way she could say anything to Karen.

'I thought you and Lawrence were getting on well,' Eve said instead.

'Lawrence seems a nice guy, but he's not my type. He sat next to me on the coach and was flirting ever so obviously, but compared to Gary, he really is dull. I mean, don't you think Gary is different from a lot of Englishmen? I so want to hear all about his life in Africa.'

'Yes, I'm sure, but be careful,' Eve said, trying to find a way to warn her without showing that she knew anything.

19

'Careful? What of?' Karen asked, baffled.

David was also giving her a funny look, so Eve tried to get out of the hole she was digging for herself without arousing suspicion.

'Oh, I don't know. Africa is a pretty dangerous place. I'm certain people don't live in the same way as they do in England. I expect Gary is all right, but you should take time to get to know him.'

'He runs a holiday company, so I can't imagine that he's involved in anything dodgy,' Karen said. 'I would love to live here — and he could be my chance.'

Eve shook her head, but decided to say nothing else in case she aroused David's suspicions. However, she couldn't help but think that Karen was heading for trouble.

Eve decided she had to find out more about Gary. She couldn't let an innocent young girl get mixed up in criminal activities. She could end up hurt — with a broken heart, or worse.

Gary suddenly appeared.

'I thought I'd come along for this. It's a while since I went on a game drive at night.'

Eve studied him. He must be at least forty, if not more; far too old for Karen, in her opinion, but she did understand the attraction. He was good-looking, with sleek dark brown hair and brown eyes, and of course, a good tan. And yes, the fact that he lived in Africa did make him exciting. However, Eve couldn't help but think that he was definitely up to no good.

They all boarded the Jeep and set off. Eve forgot about Gary as they drove into the bush, becoming excited about what they might see.

It wasn't long before they stopped and Gary spoke quietly.

'Look. It's the pride of lions we saw earlier.'

Eve was delighted. This was her first night game drive and she was thrilled. For a brief moment she thought, *To hell with whatever Gary is up to.* She had come to Africa to spend time with her new husband and to see the animals — not to chase after some criminal.

David put his arm around Eve and whispered, 'I'm so glad that you brought me here. This is already the best holiday I've ever had.'

'Mine too, darling.' Eve kissed his cheek.

She felt a little guilty. She should be directing all her attention to David, but she knew she had to find out just a little more about Gary. Karen seemed to be totally under his spell and she couldn't leave her to deal with him on her own.

She'd have to be discreet, of course. She didn't want David to know anything — but for Karen's sake, she wasn't prepared to forget about it.

At least that's what she told herself. In reality, she was desperate to know what activities Gary was involved in . . . and she was pretty sure they weren't above board.

3

The following day, the group boarded the larger Jeep and headed towards Tanzania. Eve and David were last on and had to sit at the back.

For once it was David that had held them up and Eve was none too pleased, although she didn't show it. She had wanted to sit nearer Gary at the front. Her half-hearted resolution not to get involved had faded since the previous evening. She was desperate to know more of what Gary was up to — but of course she couldn't tell David. Karen had sat behind Gary and was chatting to him. Joyce, the older lady on her own, had taken the seat next to Karen, and Lawrence was on the other side of the bus. He didn't look happy.

Kate and James were across the aisle from Eve and David. Kate spoke to them, seeming very cheerful.

'The drive was wonderful last night, wasn't it?'

'Yes, it was,' Eve replied. 'You should have come, Sophie.'

'It all sounds a bit scary to me. The daytime one was quite enough.'

Eve wondered why Sophie had come on a safari holiday if that was how she felt. She had been relatively excited the day before, but now she seemed to have turned into a timid mouse. Eve's initial liking for Sophie had started to wane, and she now believed that Kate was probably more on her wavelength.

Gary suddenly spoke up.

'Well, I hope you all enjoyed your stay at Taita Hills. We will be crossing the border this morning into Tanzania and will have lunch in Arusha. Then it's a long drive to Lake Manyara, but we will get there well in time for dinner.'

Eve thought how pleasant Gary sounded, but she knew there was something off with him. She decided to try and sit close to him at lunch and attempt to find out more. She didn't think David would be suspicious of her actions. He knew that she liked to be the centre of attention, and what better way than by getting to know the guide?

★   ★   ★

They were all seated around one big table for lunch. Eve had managed to plonk herself next to Gary as planned. She saw Karen give her a dirty look. Eve didn't care one bit. She was doing this for Karen's good, after all.

When everyone had placed their orders, Eve turned to Gary.

'So, how long have you been a tour guide, Gary?' she asked.

'Three years.'

'And what did you do before that?'

'I was in the army,' he replied.

'Really! A very different career, then?'

'Yes, it was.'

'Where were you stationed?' Eve felt as if she was squeezing blood out of a stone.

'Oh, here and there.'

'Must be difficult for your family with you being away so much.'

'I'm divorced.'

Well, at least there was that. Karen wouldn't end up having a relationship with a married man — if Gary was telling the truth, of course.

'You enjoy living in Africa, then?'

'It's my home.'

Eve decided she'd probably got as much out of him as she could, for the moment at least, so she gave up and looked around. Lawrence had managed to sit next to Karen and was chatting away. Karen seemed to be nodding in the right places, but Eve could tell she was bored.

Eve's eyes then rested on Joan, who took that opportunity to speak to her.

'Eve, I would have thought that you would have wanted a honeymoon alone with your husband, not to be stuck with a group of people? I mean, it's not that romantic.'

Eve was annoyed that Joan had

commented on her choice of honey-moon, and was reminded even more of Betty, but she answered politely. She was not going to let that woman get the better of her.

'We're having a week in Mombasa at the end of the safari. There will be time for romance then.'

Joan didn't seem able to find a response and turned away, to Eve's relief. How dare that woman make comments about them? Joan didn't know anything about her.

Eve decided it might be best to start a general conversation and spoke a little more loudly.

'This vegetable pilau is absolutely delicious. They do excellent vegetarian food here.'

'You're a vegetarian!' Joan piped up. 'No wonder you're so skinny.'

Eve glared, but said nothing. She decided Joan wasn't worth bothering about. In her opinion, she had the perfect figure; slim and toned, but certainly not underweight.

David whispered in her ear.

'I'm proud of you, Eve. You haven't risen to Joan's bait.'

Eve smiled at her new husband. She knew she was lucky to have met him. As for Joan, she was just an interfering old biddy and she couldn't be bothered to argue with her.

* * *

The ride to Lake Manyara was long, and Eve found herself dropping off to sleep. She put her head on David's chest and he put his arm around her. She snuggled up to him, feeling happy and secure. All thoughts of Gary were fading. Whatever he was up to had nothing to do with her and it was better not to get involved. This was the start of her new life with David, which should include not having secrets.

When Eve awoke a couple of hours later, they were approaching the lodge at Lake Manyara. She stretched and looked out of the window. She was looking forward to this visit. There were tree-climbing lions and she hoped they would get to see some on their early-morning drive next day.

For this evening, however, it was drinks and another amazing dinner. Eve couldn't believe how much of the food was vegetarian and how delicious it was. Quite a few of the dishes were spicy, which she loved. It was such a welcome change from Greek vegetarian food.

4

Very early the following morning, everyone was waiting outside for their transport into the park — everyone, that was, except for Lawrence.

'Where is that man?' Gary demanded, sounding quite irate. 'Everyone was told to be here by six o'clock at the latest. The best game can be seen early and late in the day.'

'I'll go and knock at his door,' Eve volunteered. 'His room is next to ours.'

'Thanks, Eve,' Gary said, sounding a little less annoyed. 'The rest of you, we'll only wait a short time for Lawrence.'

Eve thought that Gary sounded more like the man she had heard talking to Hamisi, not the helpful tour guide he sometimes was. There were definitely two sides to his personality.

A few minutes later, Eve came back.

30

'No joy, I'm afraid. I knocked loudly, and called out, but he didn't answer.'

'Well, he can stay in bed and waste this great opportunity.' Gary spoke again, sounding cross.

David was a little surprised to hear him still speaking angrily in front of the group. Weren't holiday guides supposed to keep a smile on their faces at all times?

As they walked towards the Jeep, Karen sidled up to Eve.

'Gary is so forceful, isn't he?'

'Well, that's one way of describing him. I can think of a lot of words which are more suitable.'

'You don't like him, do you, Eve?'

'I didn't say that. I just think he's hiding something.'

'Oh, nonsense,' Karen said. 'We had a lovely chat in the bar last night. He told me all about himself.'

Eve thought that whatever Gary said was probably a pack of lies, but she decided to keep the peace. Karen might be young, but she was still a grown woman and should be allowed to make her own decisions.

Sitting behind Eve and David in the Jeep were Kate and James. Eve turned round to talk to them.

'Are you enjoying the holiday?' Eve asked.

'Oh yes, it's been wonderful,' Kate said, 'and I'm sure it will get even better once we get into the Serengeti. Have you two been on safari before?'

'I have — Kenya, Botswana and Namibia. I love Africa,' Eve said. 'This is David's first time.'

'Eve persuaded me to come for our honeymoon and I'm so glad she did. I'm loving it already.'

Eve squeezed David's hand. She felt a great sense of satisfaction that she had done something to please her new husband.

'This is our first time,' Kate said. 'I don't know why we left it so long to come.'

'Look over to the left, there's an elephant,' Gary shouted out.

Eve's breath was taken away. She had feared they might not see any elephants because of the poaching, but there was one right in front of the Jeep. Everyone got their cameras out.

'He's truly amazing,' James said.

Sophie, however, wasn't so keen.

'What if he rams our Jeep? We could be killed.'

Eve had changed her mind about Sophie. She wasn't really friendship material at all.

'Why did you come on this safari, Sophie? You don't seem to be enjoying it,' she commented, trying to sound relaxed and not as annoyed as she was beginning to feel.

'Richard has always wanted to come. He does so many things I like to do, so it's only fair.'

Eve started to change her mind yet again. Relationships had to be give and take.

After they had passed the elephant, a group of warthogs trundled along and then there was the sight Eve most wanted to see here; the tree-climbing lions. Everyone got out their cameras and there was lots of clicking as the animals dozed in the heat.

'That Lawrence was a bit stupid missing this, don't you think, Gary?' Joan remarked.

'Well, perhaps he's not well,' Eve piped up.

'Wouldn't stop me. I've come a long way to see all this.'

Eve didn't bother saying anything else. She had decided that Joan was an unpleasant woman and wasn't worth taking any notice of.

★　★　★

Everyone went straight to breakfast when they returned from their game drive. Eve noticed that Karen went and sat with Gary. They were laughing and Eve couldn't help but worry. She couldn't get his words out of her mind. He could be prepared to kill somebody.

There was, however, no point telling

Karen that. Either she might not believe her or she might confront Gary, and then all hell could break loose.

Finishing their breakfast, Eve and David headed off to their room. As they were approaching their door, they heard a loud scream.

'That's coming from Lawrence's room,' Eve exclaimed. 'Come on, David, let's go.'

Eve almost ran, the screams still resounding through the air. David followed her quickly.

Lawrence's door was open and Eve dashed in. A maid stood blocking their view of the bed.

'What is it?' Eve asked the girl, who was trembling.

'The man. He is dead, I think.'

Lawrence lay sprawled on his back, his neck slashed, blood all over the sheets and his nightclothes. Eve thought she was going to be sick. Yes, she had discovered a dead body before — that of Lucy Fowler a couple of years previously on Crete — but it wasn't as gory as this.

David came up behind Eve and gasped.

'He's dead, David. Someone has slashed his throat.'

'What are we going to do?' the maid asked. She had stopped screaming, but was still shaking.

Eve had regained her composure.

'Don't worry, I'll find someone to help. You'd better wait here as you found the body.'

The girl nodded, even though the last thing she wanted to do was to remain in the room.

'Gary was still having breakfast when we left. I'll see if he's still there,' Eve said. 'You stay here with the girl.'

David nodded, even though all he wanted to do was scream out 'Not again'. How could they come all the way out to Africa and be confronted with a murder? Because this was definitely murder; there was no doubt about it, and Eve being Eve was bound to want to get involved.

Eve dashed down into the dining area and was pleased to see that Gary was still there.

'I'm so relieved you're here, Gary. Something awful has happened.'

Gary had been engrossed in conversation with Karen and looked annoyed at being disturbed.

'It's rude to interrupt,' he said, frowning.

Gary had already decided that Eve was trouble. She was nosey, and seemed to want to run things.

'Well, I'm sorry to disturb your little tête à tête, but somebody has murdered Lawrence Brady. I think that is a good enough reason for me to interrupt you.'

Gary almost spat out his coffee.

'What do you mean? Murdered? Who on earth would want to murder him? Are you sure?'

'Well, a slit throat and blood everywhere indicate that he is dead,' Eve replied sarcastically.

She didn't like Gary's attitude towards her. He was condescending and she felt like having a go at him. However, for once she kept her cool.

'Did you find him?' Gary asked, calming down.

'No, a maid did. We heard her scream.'

Karen's face was as white as a sheet.

'Are you all right, Karen?' she asked.

'I can't believe this. I wasn't very nice to him and now he's dead. I feel so bad.'

'Come on, Karen,' Gary said. 'He was forcing his attentions on you. He didn't get the message that you weren't interested.'

Karen tried to smile, while Eve thought that Gary was exaggerating. Lawrence had only chatted with Karen and perhaps flirted a little.

'Well, this is all good and well, but what about Lawrence?' Eve pressed.

'I had better go to his room and then I'll ring the police,' Gary said. 'It'll take a while for them to get here, so we won't be moving on to the Serengeti any time soon.'

Gary got up and left, giving Karen a kiss on the cheek. Eve felt things were progressing too quickly between them, but perhaps this tragedy might slow things down a bit.

Eve sat down next to Karen.

'Can I get you something? You look as if you're in shock.'

'I could do with a brandy, but I suppose it's too early for that.'

'Come up to my room. I've got some Metaxa, a Greek brandy. It'll do you the power of good.'

'Will I have to go by Lawrence's room?'

'No, it's on the other side of ours.'

The two women went to Eve's room, where she poured them both a measure of Metaxa. Eve felt she needed one as well.

A few minutes later, David came in.

'Bit early to start drinking, isn't it?' he said.

'It's medicinal. It's all been a bit of a shock.'

'I know. Gary came in and was quite

taken aback at seeing Lawrence the way he is.'

Eve remembered Gary's words the night before. He didn't seem to have a problem with getting rid of people. Perhaps he was the one who had killed Lawrence! They had acted as if they didn't know each other, but that could just be a front. Perhaps Lawrence had known something damning about Gary and was threatening to expose him.

Eve didn't know what to do. The police were bound to come along soon and they would all be questioned. Should she tell them what she had heard Gary say to Hamisi, or should she keep her mouth shut? Gary could be involved in some really shady activities and he might not hesitate to kill anyone who got in his way . . . including her.

5

Everybody was gathered in the lobby of the lodge, ready to go on to the next step of the safari. They were chatting, and it seemed they were all looking forward to going to the Serengeti.

Eve wondered why nobody was talking about Lawrence and his brutal murder, but then it dawned on her that they didn't know what had happened. She didn't want to be the one to break the bad news, and was relieved when Gary came along and told them that Lawrence was dead.

Nobody said a word for a few moments. Eve imagined that they were all in a state of shock, and that it would hit them soon enough. Then they would probably talk about nothing else.

Sophie was the first to speak. She looked distressed and was almost in tears.

'This is terrible. I want to go home. I thought the animals were dangerous, but now there seems to be a crazed killer on the loose. Come on, Richard, let's get out of here.'

'That won't be possible,' Gary said quickly. 'The police will want to speak to all of you. I imagine they will treat everyone as a suspect.'

'That's ridiculous.' Joan spoke crossly. 'Why on earth would anyone of us want to murder Lawrence Brady? Ken and I had never set eyes on the man before this holiday.'

'That's right,' Ken said, for once managing to get a word in. 'This is nothing to do with us.'

'Well, try and leave then. How far do you think you'll get? We are in a game park after all.' Gary spoke impatiently, then realising that this news was a shock to everyone, put on a softer tone.

'It'll only be routine. Once you have satisfied the police with your answers, we will be able to travel on to the Serengeti.'

'But I want to go home,' Sophie wailed.

'Oh, for God's sake, Sophie, shut up!' Richard snapped. 'I don't ask much of you, but a safari is the one thing I've wanted to do for a long time. You know that. Anyway, why ever would anyone want to kill you? I doubt if we're in any danger — nor have we anything to hide, have we, Sophie?'

She looked at him meekly and said no more.

Eve studied Richard and Sophie. For a couple married only a year, they were not a happy partnership. She wondered again how she could possibly have thought that she and Sophie could be friends.

★   ★   ★

It was a good couple of hours before the police arrived. During that time, nobody said much. There was some whispering between couples, but generally the mood was sombre.

Eve noticed Joan getting restless. Eventually, the older woman broke the awkward silence.

'Are we going to get to the Serengeti today, Gary? We paid a lot of money for this trip and I didn't expect it to end up like this.'

'I don't suppose Lawrence wanted the trip to end up like this for him either, Joan,' Eve snapped. 'I think we should show a little respect.'

'Thank you, Eve,' Gary said, surprising her with his friendly tone. 'Mrs Ferguson, we will do our best to resume the safari with as little change to the itinerary as possible. However, we may end up having to stay here one more night and then set off for the Serengeti in the early morning.'

'Humph. I think I will complain about this when I get back to England. I will also be mentioning you, Gary. You haven't really been very helpful.'

'That's your prerogative, madam, but you should know I am one of the company owners.'

Joan stared at him sullenly. There was little else she could say.

'She really is an obnoxious woman,' Eve whispered to David.

'You're not wrong there.'

'She keeps reminding me of Betty. It wouldn't surprise me if they were related.'

David couldn't help but smile. Eve and Betty had been at loggerheads from the moment they had set eyes on each other.

Their conversation came to an abrupt end with the arrival of two policemen. Gary went over to speak to them, but came back quickly.

'The police are going to look at the body and then they will question you all one by one.'

'Can't we be seen in couples?' Sophie asked.

'I'm afraid not,' Gary replied.

She looked very nervous and Eve thought that wouldn't go down well with the police. They could think she was hiding something.

Joan was still angry, while her husband looked as if he was in another world. Eve thought he probably switched off when his wife started ranting. Kate and James didn't look too fazed by the situation, nor did Joyce. Karen, sitting next to Eve, was very quiet. Eve imagined she was scared of talking to the police.

It wasn't long before the two officers came back. They asked Gary to come with them and Eve guessed he was going for his interview.

Gary wasn't long and he told Eve to go and talk to the police next. Eve felt a wave of excitement sweep over her. She wondered how different it would be to be interviewed by the African police. She had got so used to Dimitris Kastrinakis back on Crete, and she knew how to handle him — or so she thought. These Tanzanian officers were probably a completely different kettle of fish.

Eve went into the room allocated for the interviews. The two officers looked grim, so she probably shouldn't take any liberties with them.

'Sit down,' one of them said to her abruptly.

She did as she was told.

'Who are you?'

'Eve Masters.'

She watched him tick her name off on a list.

'How long have you known Lawrence Brady?'

'I only met him two days ago, when I joined this safari.'

'You are sure about this?'

Eve was annoyed. Did they think she was lying?

'Of course I'm sure,' she replied, a little too abruptly. The officer gave her a severe look.

'When did you last see the deceased alive?'

'Last night, at about eleven, in the bar.'

'Did you speak with him?'

'No. I've hardly spoken to him at all.'

'And did you see him alive this morning?'

'No. He didn't come on the game drive which left at six. When we got back, we had breakfast and then I headed over to my room with my husband. We heard screams from Lawrence's room, rushed in and found a maid in there. She had discovered Lawrence dead.'

'What time was this?'

'Around nine.'

Eve wished one of the officers would smile. They looked so serious, and she felt guilty even though she hadn't done anything wrong.'

'Is there anything else you can tell us?'

Eve hesitated, wondering whether she should tell them what she had heard Gary say two nights previously, but changed her mind. It probably had nothing to do with Lawrence's death, so why make more trouble? She felt that there was something very dark about Gary and she didn't want to get on the wrong side of him.

'That will be all for now,' the inspector said.

Eve got up to go. She was relieved it was all over. The police, with their sharp manner, certainly made her feel guilty. Perhaps they might catch the killer sooner rather than later.

The others went in one by one. The consensus was that Lawrence had been seen alive at around eleven the previous night, but not after.

'All right, everybody,' Gary said after speaking to the officers again. 'We are free to go to the Serengeti.'

'Thank heavens,' Joan remarked. 'I mean, why would anybody here want to kill Lawrence? We've only just met him. Those policemen certainly made me feel guilty, though.'

'It was awful,' Sophie said, her voice wobbling. 'I really struggled to stop myself from crying.'

Richard put an arm around his wife. He seemed to have forgiven her for her earlier outburst.

'Right then, we leave in half an hour,'

Gary said. 'Go and get your bags and freshen up if you need to. I'll meet you outside shortly.'

6

The drive to the lodge in the Serengeti was a long and dusty one. However, as they had to travel through the reserve to get to their lodge, they had a chance to see some wildlife en route.

There were plenty of zebra, as well as impala and other members of the deer family. They were even lucky enough to spot a couple of elephants.

The group stopped for lunch at a restaurant overlooking the Ngorongoro Crater. The view was fabulous and Eve was excited. She couldn't wait to go into the crater on their way back from the Serengeti. There was supposed to be a large concentration of animals there, including all of the Big Five — elephant, rhinoceros, leopard, buffalo and lions.

The sombre mood started to lift as the group saw more wildlife, and even

Joan looked happier. Eve, however, couldn't stop returning to what she had overheard Gary saying to Hamisi.

Perhaps he and Lawrence were connected in some way, and had just pretended not to know each other? Lawrence may have had something on Gary which could destroy him. If Gary really was prepared to kill an employee of his, he could just as easily have killed Lawrence.

Perhaps she should have told the police, but if Gary had deflected police questions, she might have created a noose for her own neck.

Arriving at the lodge, everyone went straight to their rooms to shower and change. It had been a long day and they all wanted to freshen up.

Entering their room, Eve collapsed on the bed. The day had been a strain and she wished it were over. She couldn't tell David, but she had been agonising over Gary's threats.

Still, a long cold gin and tonic and a good meal might help revive her spirits.

'Are you all right, Eve?' David asked. 'You've been very quiet all day. It's not like you.'

'I keep seeing Lawrence's body,' Eve said. 'It was so gruesome — not at all like Lucy Fowler's.'

Eve was lying, despite the fact that she had promised herself that she wouldn't lie to David again. She wanted to tell him the truth; that all that was on her mind were Gary's words, but she couldn't. He'd say she should have told the police — but if she told them now, they would ask why she hadn't volunteered the information before.

'I know, darling,' David replied. 'It was horrible, but we've got to put it behind us.'

Eve got up off the bed and kissed David. He was so reassuring and she knew she was lucky to have found him. He still made her tingle all over when he touched her. They had been a couple for almost three years, and she found him more exciting now than ever before.

'You're right, David. Let's just enjoy our honeymoon. We'd better get freshened up quickly as there's a gin and tonic with my name on it in the bar.'

* * *

Dinner was a wonderful affair for Eve. She was revelling in the great choice of vegetarian food. This evening, she and David both had coconut bean soup to start. They then had ugali — cornmeal — served with a vegetable stew for Eve, and chicken for David. They both ended up with delicious fried bananas.

Kate and James joined Eve and David at their table, to Eve's delight. She had decided they were a lovely couple. She would have hated to sit with Joan and Ken, and Sophie's whining would get on her nerves.

Eve noticed Karen and Joyce sitting together. Karen looked as if she had been crying. There was no sign of Gary.

'What an extraordinary day it's been,' James said. 'And it must have been worse for you two — seeing the body, I mean.'

'You seem to be bearing up, though,' Kate added.

'No, it wasn't nice at all, but we are trying to clear our minds of it,' Eve said.

'Yes — you must. You don't want your honeymoon to be ruined.'

'No chance of that,' David said. 'Seeing all those animals on our way here cheered us up.'

'I'm so glad we saw elephants again,' Kate said. 'Like you, Eve, I was worried that we wouldn't see any with all the poaching that's going on.'

'It's disgusting,' Eve said, her voice full of emotion. 'There should be the harshest penalties for poachers. I know what I'd like to do to them.'

'Eve loves animals so much. You may have noticed,' David said.

'Yes — you're a vegetarian, aren't you?' James asked Eve.

'We have toyed with the idea,' Kate added. 'But we haven't taken the plunge yet. Mind you, the vegetarian food we've had here is delicious. I think we've eaten more vegetables than meat.'

The conversation continued and Eve found herself forgetting about Gary and Lawrence.

'Who's up for a nightcap, then?' James asked.

'I think we are, aren't we, David?'

David nodded. He'd had such a nice evening and didn't want it to end just yet. It was so pleasant to have Eve in such a relaxed mood. He had been worried when they saw Lawrence's body. Wouldn't she want to get involved as usual?

David hoped that his wife was thinking that she was out of her depth here. The police hadn't been at all friendly and were nothing like Dimitris Kastrinakis and his crew. Dimitris would get cross with Eve and tell her off, but he was approachable. However, little did he know of the turmoil which had been going through Eve's mind that day.

As they entered the bar, Eve stopped dead. Gary was sitting with another man — none other than the man she had seen in his office when she overheard them talking. Wasn't his name Hamisi — and why on earth was he here? They must be up to something, but Eve couldn't fathom what.

7

The following morning, everyone was up early to go on their first game drive in the Serengeti. Eve was so looking forward to this; all thoughts about the murder of Lawrence Brady evaporating, if only temporarily.

David had picked up on Eve's excitement and they were both hoping to see the migration of the wildebeest, which happened in June. Their timing was perfect, or so Eve hoped.

Gary arrived looking tired and Eve's mind was whisked back to the events of the past couple of days. She couldn't shake the feeling that their safari trip had somehow got embroiled in their guide's shady activities.

As they got into the Jeep, Karen made sure she got a seat next to Gary. Eve wished she could warn her against him, but it would mean telling her what she had heard, and she couldn't trust Karen. She would probably rush straight to Gary and repeat what Eve had told her. If Gary knew she had overheard him say that he might get rid of someone, her own life could be put in danger.

Eve started to relax again when the Jeep left the lodge and they started to see wild animals. There was a majestic leopard up a tree, a few jackals, more zebra, another pride of lions with some gorgeous cubs, and Eve's favourite, the cheetah. They all watched in awe as the cheetah got up and sped off through the Serengeti. Eve wondered what it must be to run like the wind.

There was no sign of wildebeest, but they were spending quite a few days here, so there was still the possibility of seeing them.

Everybody clicked away on their cameras and the worries of the previous day seemed to have left the group . . . everyone, that is, except for Eve.

On returning to the lodge, David went to lie down as he was tired after the early start. Eve decided to sunbathe and chose a lounger by the swimming pool. She closed her eyes, hoping to have a short nap, but she couldn't sleep. Although she had thoroughly enjoyed the game drive, images of Lawrence Brady's body now filled her mind.

It took a lot to frighten Eve, but the sight of him lying with his throat cut wouldn't go away. Whoever had killed him was vicious and cruel. She couldn't imagine anyone in their party committing such a terrible act — not even Joan. However, Gary seemed to fit the bill perfectly.

After about half an hour, Karen came and took the sunbed next to Eve's.

'I'm not taking David's bed, am I?'

'No, he's resting in our room.'

'I'm tired too, but I'm desperate to get a tan.'

'Well, be careful, the sun is pretty hot here.'

'I know. I've put plenty of sun cream on. You do have a lovely tan, Eve.'

'Well, it comes from living on Crete. The weather is good there for a large part of the year. You find that you don't need to sunbathe for that long to keep up a tan.'

'Can I tell you a secret, Eve?' Karen asked.

'Yes, of course. I'll be the soul of discretion.'

Eve didn't know if she was excited to hear her secret, or dreading it. However, as soon as Karen spoke, she knew exactly how she felt.

'Well, Gary kissed me last night.'

'Oh,' Eve said, determining not to be too harsh with Karen. It was none of her business, but she was still concerned. 'That's what you wanted, isn't it?' she said, trying to be diplomatic.

'I thought it was. Well, it is, but your words have stuck in the back of my mind, especially as I saw him just a little while ago arguing with somebody. He actually grabbed the man's arm. I thought he was going to break it.'

Eve wondered if the man Karen had seen with Gary was Hamisi. He had mysteriously reappeared here, and Gary had been locked in a deep conversation with him the previous night.

'Well, I'd be careful, Karen. I know you like him, but take your time to get to know him.'

'I haven't got much time. If I want him to ask me to stay here with him, he'll have to fall for me pretty hard, and quickly.'

'Are you sure you want to give up everything in England, especially your friends and family, to come to a strange country? It's probably a lot more lawless here than the UK.'

'Yes, no, I don't know.' Karen looked confused. 'I'm sure my parents will be upset and I'll miss them and my friends, but I hate my job.'

'What would you do here, though? You'll get bored when Gary is taking out safari groups.'

'He might get me a job in his company. In fact, I'm pretty sure he would.'

Eve thought Karen was a little naïve. For all they knew, Gary could flirt with lots of single women on these safaris. However, she knew it wasn't her place to dash all of Karen's hopes and dreams.

Then Eve was struck with an idea. She could do an internet search on Gary and see if she could find out more about him.

Why not search Lawrence as well? She might find a connection between them. It didn't cross her mind that the police might already have done this and could be on their way to arresting the guilty party.

*   *   *

In the early evening, most of the group gathered in the bar. Eve was surprised that Karen decided to sit with her and

David rather than wait for Gary, but perhaps she was now a little scared of him. Eve hoped so. She had looked him up on the internet, but all she could find were details of his safari business. If he was involved in something shady, he was probably keeping it quiet.

As for Lawrence, he had turned out to be a reporter for one of the national newspapers. Eve couldn't think of a connection between the two, unless Lawrence had got wind of something Gary was up to. She felt deflated, having hoped to find some reason for Gary to have killed Lawrence.

They were joined in the bar by Kate and James, but Sophie and Richard sat on their own, as did Joan and Ken. Joyce hadn't come in yet and nor had Gary.

Everyone at Eve's table chatted about the game drives that day, telling each other what their favourite parts had been. Eve noticed Karen was a little distracted and thought that she must be thinking about Gary. He was nowhere to be seen.

The other two couples were very quiet, but Eve had no inclination to ask either to join them. Joan was obnoxious and Sophie whined too much.

Then Gary entered the bar and went to order a drink. Once he had it, he looked around and headed for Eve's table.

'You don't mind if I join you?' he asked politely.

To Eve's surprise, Karen spoke quickly.

'Of course not. Come and sit next to me.'

Gary did so and then took a long swig of his whisky and soda.

'I hope that today has made up for the traumatic events of yesterday,' he said.

'Yes, they have,' Eve answered. 'It's been a wonderful day.'

How much friendlier he seemed, compared to the other day at lunch when she had tried to find out more about him.

'You enjoy your job, then?' she asked.

'I love it. I never get tired of seeing animals in the wild.'

'You're so lucky, Gary,' Karen said. 'I wish I could do something like your job.'

'There's nothing stopping you, Karen. The world's your oyster.'

Karen smiled dreamily at him. Eve was disappointed. Karen must have got over her worries about Gary.

Then, all of a sudden, the two policemen who had interviewed everybody at Lake Manyara strode in, looking ready for business. They headed straight for Eve's table.

One of the policemen, whom Eve reckoned must be the chief inspector as he was the one who had done most of the talking during her interview, looked straight at Gary.

'Mr Gary Brown, we are here to question you again about the murder of Mr Lawrence Brady.'

'Why? I said everything I had to say back at Lake Manyara.'

'We now have evidence that could implicate you in Mr Brady's murder. Come this way, please.'

Gary got up, knowing there was no point in resisting. He didn't look afraid. Perhaps he had been in this position before.

Eve looked at Karen. She had gone as white as a sheet, and Eve had to resist an urge to say *I told you so.*

No one said anything until the police and Gary had left the room. Then Joan piped up.

'Can this holiday get any worse? What's going to happen to us now if he's arrested?'

'Shut up, you old bat,' Karen shouted. 'Gary's only been taken away for questioning. I know he's innocent and they'll let him go. There can't be any solid evidence that he killed Lawrence.'

'How dare you call me names, you stupid child! I've seen you with him, hanging on every word. He's much too old for you and you're just making a fool of yourself.'

'I'm not. He's fallen for me, I know he has.'

'Everybody,' Eve said. 'Let's not fight amongst ourselves. I'm sure there's been some mistake and Gary will be back with us shortly.'

Eve didn't really think that there was a mistake, but she wanted to quieten everyone down. There was no point in them bickering with each other.

'How would you know?' Joan spoke viciously. 'You seem to think you're better than us.'

'Joan, there is no need to have a go at me. I think we should all have another drink and wait to see what happens. I'm sure that if Gary is arrested, we will be provided with another guide.'

'Yes, Eve's right,' James put in. 'There's no need to start worrying too much.'

'I paid good money for this holiday,' Joan continued, not wanting to be put off track. 'I shall certainly be asking for a refund.'

'This is the worst holiday I've ever been on,' Sophie wailed. 'I want to go home.'

'Well, if you do, you'll be going on your own,' Richard replied.

'How can you be so cruel, Richard? I thought you loved me.'

With tears streaming down her cheeks, Sophie rushed out of the bar. Richard didn't follow her. Instead, he went to get himself a drink.

Joan and Ken also left, saying that they were going to dinner. David went up to the bar to get drinks and asked Richard to join their table.

'I can't believe Gary is a murderer,' Karen said mutinously.

'He's probably not,' Eve replied, trying to reassure her new friend, but thinking inside that he could very well be a killer.

When David came back with their gin and tonics, he whispered in her ear.

'I'm very proud of you, Eve. You did well quietening everyone down. Not to mention the fact that you've kept out of the murder inquiry. I admit I was worried about what you might do.'

'Well, I did promise you I wouldn't do anything dangerous again, darling.'

Eve kissed David and had a long drink of her gin and tonic. She felt guilt envelop her. She hadn't really done much to interfere, but she had tried to find out more about Gary and Lawrence . . . and she was desperate to find out who the killer was.

*   *   *

Gary sat opposite the two detectives, looking calm and sure of himself.

'Somebody saw you enter Mr Brady's room at around five-thirty yesterday morning,' the chief inspector, Abasi, said.

'Who saw me?'

'A member of the lodge's staff.'

'They're not usually around the bedrooms at that time of the morning. Who was it anyway?'

'I think that is our business. They all

know you at that lodge, so this person can be trusted.'

'Some people working at that lodge don't like me so they could be lying. Anyway, why on earth would I want to murder this man? I barely knew him.' Gary's voice was rising.

He was growing nervous. If someone was trying to frame him, what could he do? The police were more likely to believe a native than a foreigner.

'Mr Brady was a reporter. He could have got wind of the fact that you organise hunts.'

'How? I use a different name for my hunting business. How would he have put two and two together? Anyway, my hunts are all legal.'

'That may be so, but many people don't like it, especially with all the animals that are being poached. We think Mr Brady wanted to expose you. It would be a great story. Safari tour guide also runs hunts to kill the animals he proudly shows to holidaymakers.'

'Got to make a living somehow,'

Gary said carelessly.

The inspector slammed his fist on the table.

'You will spend the night here under armed guard, so don't try to escape. Very early in the morning we travel to Dar Es Salaam.'

'Fine, but I don't think that you will have enough evidence to convict me.'

'We'll see about that.'

★   ★   ★

Everyone went into dinner, and apart from Joan and Ken, all sat at a big table. Sophie hadn't come back since running off and Richard showed no inclination to go and fetch her.

'This is awful,' Karen said as soon as they were all settled. 'I can't believe that Gary would kill anyone.'

'I don't mean to be harsh,' Kate said. 'But you don't really know him that well.'

'But why would he want to kill Lawrence? It doesn't make sense.'

'Perhaps they did know each other,' Eve remarked. 'Possibly Lawrence was threatening him and Gary decided to get rid of him.'

'No — I won't believe that, I just won't.'

Eve was worried about Karen. She was already too deeply involved with Gary, and she couldn't help but think that the possibility of him being the killer was quite high.

It was a buffet that evening, so they all went up to choose their food. Once again, Eve was impressed by the number of mouthwatering vegetarian dishes on offer.

As they were eating, Adhama, their driver, came in. He went to Eve's table, but called Joan and Ken over.

'I think you know that Gary has been arrested. I have contacted my head office and they will be sending another tour guide tomorrow.'

'It's a long way. Does this mean we will miss our game drives tomorrow morning?' Joan asked. 'This really is the worst holiday I have ever — '

Adhama ignored her rude remarks.

'I will take you on a drive in the morning. Hopefully, your new guide will be here in the afternoon.'

'We paid for a tour guide, not just a driver. You do know that?' Joan demanded.

'It's hardly Adhama's fault,' Eve said crossly to Joan and then spoke to the driver. 'Adhama, that's fine. We'll all enjoy a game drive with you tomorrow morning.'

Adhama smiled at Eve.

'Thank you, madam; I will see you in the morning at six.'

'Nicely said, Eve,' David whispered in her ear.

He was proud of Eve. She hadn't interfered in the murder, plus she had tried to keep the peace. She could really have had a go at Joan, but she had been very restrained.

'I can be diplomatic sometimes.' Eve smiled.

'Oh — there's Gary with the police!'

Karen cried out. 'I have to speak to him.

'No!' Kate and Eve shouted in unison.

However, it was too late. Karen had already rushed out of the dining room.

'Gary! I know you didn't do it.'

'Thank you, Karen,' was all he could get out before the policemen shoved him away from her.

Karen came back into the dining room.

'It's awful. They just pushed poor Gary away. They barely let me speak to him.'

Eve put her arm around Karen. It looked as if the girl had fallen for Gary hook, line, and sinker.

She couldn't criticise her for that. After all, she had fallen for David the first time that she had seen him, and look at them now. They were happily married and she was more in love with him than ever before.

8

The following morning, everybody stood outside the lodge waiting for Adhama — everyone, that was, apart from Joan and Ken.

'Well,' Eve said to David. 'I see Joan and Ken haven't bothered coming.'

'They could just be late.'

'Humph. I'm sure they're just being awkward. They'll probably miss out on a great drive.'

'Or you're hoping they will.'

Eve just smiled and said nothing.

'Well, it's ten past six,' Adhama said. 'I'm sorry, but we must go. We cannot wait any longer for the other people.'

Nobody put up any objection, not even Joyce, who had started to get friendly with Joan and Ken.

They all piled into the Jeep and went out for their game drive. It turned out to be a good one, and Eve was secretly pleased that Joan had missed it. It served her right for being so negative.

The highlight was seeing hundreds of wildebeest migrating. Eve could hardly believe that she had got to see this — and particularly that Joan hadn't.

'Eve, stop smiling,' David said. 'I know exactly what you're thinking. You're glad that Joan has missed this, aren't you?'

'You know me too well, David. I'm sorry, but I can't completely change the way I am.'

'I don't think I'd want you to lose the spirit you have, darling.'

He put his arm around Eve and she rested her head on his shoulder. For that one moment, she forgot all about the murder.

The group then went to the hippo pool, their first viewing of these enormous creatures. Nobody could believe how many there were in just one place. Eve was fascinated, but knew how dangerous they could be.

They all got out of the Jeep as the

pool was way below them. Sophie, however, gave it a miss. Eve noticed her eyes looked puffy and she and Richard hadn't exchanged a word on the drive. Eve wondered why she had come that morning. She looked as if she was hating every minute.

As time went on, they saw lions, baboons, hyenas, warthogs and vultures, plus the now familiar zebra. Eve was relieved that so far they hadn't seen any of the predators kill other animals. She didn't like to think about this, but she knew it was nature and that was the only way some animals could survive.

* * *

On returning to the lodge, who should be sitting in the lobby, but Joan. She stormed up to Adhama.

'How dare you go without us?' she screamed.

Adhama seemed calm as he replied, 'You weren't here at the agreed time. In fact it was ten past six when we left. We gave you ten minutes.'

'I'll complain about you, mark my words.'

Adhama shrugged and said nothing. Who would she complain to? Gary had been arrested and the other owner of the holiday company lived in America and had very little to do with the day-to-day running of the business.

'Joan, you really are a horrible person,' Eve exclaimed. 'You were late so don't expect the rest of us, who were here on time, to wait for you.

'Adhama is doing his best. He's probably upset that Gary has been arrested, so you should be more sensitive. Anyway, we had a fantastic game drive. We saw lots of hippo which, as you know, we hadn't seen before today. And the highlight was the migration of the wildebeest. Bet you're sorry to have missed that.'

David shook his head. There was the old Eve. No, he didn't want her to lose her spirit, but she could go too far sometimes. The atmosphere often ended up pretty awkward.

Eve, however, didn't wait for Joan to reply but instead marched into the dining room, followed by everyone else. Nobody looked at Joan. In truth, most of them felt the same as Eve, but didn't have the nerve to speak in the way Eve had.

As they tucked into their breakfast, David was relieved to see that Joan hadn't come in. She'd probably had breakfast while they were out on the game drive. However, he was surprised that she hadn't followed Eve to give her a piece of her mind. Perhaps Joan wasn't as confident as she seemed.

★   ★   ★

Eve and David went up to their room after breakfast. Following her confrontation with Joan, she had calmed down, and started to think about Gary again. Had it been a mistake not to tell the police about what he had said?

She decided she had to confess to

David. He wouldn't be happy — even though she was resisting getting involved. However, she steeled herself and started to speak.

'David, I have something to tell you.'

'That sounds ominous,' he replied.

She had always sounded like this when she had got involved in crimes. Surely that couldn't be the case here?

'Back at Taita Hills,' Eve continued nervously, 'I overheard Gary talk to another man, someone called Hamisi. He said something about getting rid of someone if that person didn't do what was expected of him.'

'Oh Eve, why didn't you tell me?'

'Because you never want me to get involved in crimes, do you?'

David shook his head. He knew she was right. He didn't want her to be concerned with matters which were better left to the police.

'I know, Eve, I'm sorry. I take it that you didn't tell the police?'

'I decided against it. I mean, Gary might not have intended that he was going to murder someone, although it did sound like it. I admit I was a little afraid as well. Goodness only knows what Gary's involved in. Plus it doesn't seem logical that he would kill Lawrence. I mean, why?'

'I think you should tell the police now, Eve.'

'It's too late. They'll want to know why I didn't tell them earlier. I'll probably be thrown into jail.'

Eve was almost in tears by this time. All her confidence had been sapped away.

'It's OK, Eve.' David took her in his arms. 'You're probably right. I don't suppose it will make much difference now that Gary has been arrested, although if he's released, it might do.'

Eve wondered if she could ever please David. He hated it when she interfered, but the one time she had kept her mouth shut, he was reprimanding her. She loved him very much, but sometimes he could be a little contrary.

★ ★ ★

That evening, when everyone was sitting in the bar before dinner, Gary entered. Silence fell as they all stared at him. Karen's face had lit up.

Gary walked over to his group and smiled.

'I expect you're all wondering what I'm doing back here. Well, the member of staff who had supposedly seen me going into Lawrence's room has retracted her statement. She decided she had made a mistake, and it wasn't me who she had seen. She couldn't be sure who it was, but now she thinks it was a woman. I don't know why she said it was me, but for some reason she has never liked me. The police have decided that her evidence is unsound. In fact, they're not sure if she actually did see anybody go into the room at all. She has always tried to seek the limelight.'

'Gary, I'm so pleased to see you,' Karen exclaimed. 'I knew it wasn't you.'

She leapt up and threw herself into Gary's arms.

'Yes, it's nice to see you too,' he said, but after a moment he gently pushed her away.

Eve was surprised to see him acting so professionally with Karen. However, she did think this was all very fishy. Had Gary done something to this staff member which had made her want to retaliate and to hurt him? In her opinion, it was a distinct possibility. Then, to change her mind and say it was a woman was very far-fetched indeed.

David looked at Eve. She was very quiet and he knew her mind was working overtime. However, he tried to reassure himself. After all, they were in Tanzania and she might be a little reluctant to get involved with the African police. They had been quite harsh when interviewing everybody.

'This is all very unsatisfactory,' Joan declared. 'For all we know you could still be guilty, Gary, and you're expecting us to put ourselves in your hands. How come your partner has agreed to you coming back?'

'Firstly, the police have no evidence to convict me. Secondly, I own sixty per cent of the company, so it's up to me whether I come back or not. If you have any problems with this, you are welcome to leave and I will refund your money.'

Joan looked startled.

'No, it's fine,' she said after a few moments.

Eve wanted to laugh out loud. Gary had certainly put Joan in her place. Still, she wasn't entirely convinced that he hadn't killed Lawrence. She intended to keep an eye on him.

After finishing their drinks, most of the group went to dinner. Eve noticed that Karen stayed in the bar with Gary. What she would do to be a fly on the wall and hear their conversation.

★   ★   ★

'What would you like to drink, Karen?' Gary asked.

'Oh, a gin and tonic, please.'

She wasn't madly keen on gin and tonic, but she thought it made her look sophisticated — just like Eve.

'Make that two,' Gary said to the barman.

Getting their drinks, they went and sat down.

'I knew you hadn't murdered Lawrence,' Karen said for the third time.

Gary smiled at her.

'I think you were the only one in the group who believed that. I reckon that Joan would have had me thrown in to jail without a trial.'

'Oh, she's such a busybody. She's taken a dislike to Eve for some reason. I can't imagine why. I think Eve's great. She's so stylish and confident. I wish I was like her.'

'Eve seems a little overbearing to me,' Gary replied with a frown.

'Perhaps a little. She did warn me off you.'

'Me?' Gary said, sounding shocked. 'Why on earth would she do that? She doesn't even know me. I'll have to have a word with her.'

'Oh, please don't. She'll know I'll have told you. Anyway, I can make up my own mind.'

'OK, let's not discuss her. Let's talk about us.'

'There's an us?' Karen stuttered.

She was shocked. Yes, she liked Gary a lot, but she couldn't believe that he felt the same way.

'If you want there to be an us, I'm happy.'

'Oh yes — I want that more than anything.'

Gary leaned over and gave her a gentle kiss.

Karen trembled. This was the real thing. Gary was handsome, mysterious and exciting, and she was enjoying every bit of her time spent with him.

'You know people won't approve of us,' Gary continued. 'I am quite a bit older than you.'

'I don't care what people think.'

'OK — so we'll have some fun together,' Gary said easily.

Alarm bells started to ring for Karen. Was Gary just suggesting a holiday romance? However, she dismissed these thoughts quickly. She would make him fall in love with her and then he would ask her to stay in Africa with him.

* * *

Later that evening, Gary saw Eve standing alone in the bar, David having gone to their room to change his shirt as he had spilt gravy on it.

Gary walked over to Eve. Karen noticed and cringed. She wished she'd not said anything to him about Eve. Karen had grown to like her and thought of her as a role model. She didn't want their friendship jeopardised.

'Excuse me, Eve,' Gary said abruptly. 'I would appreciate it if you didn't speak badly about me to Karen. She is a grown woman, after all.'

Eve fumed. How dare he come and tell her off! They had paid good money for this holiday and deserved to be treated with respect.

'I did not speak badly of you,' she retorted, trying to keep calm, but not quite succeeding. 'I just told her to be careful. After all, she knows nothing about you.'

Eve believed Gary was trouble, but she couldn't tell him why. She wasn't going to admit to overhearing him speak to Hamisi. It might put her own life in danger.

'Still, I'd rather that you left Karen alone to make up her own mind — are we clear?'

Gary walked off without waiting for an answer, leaving Eve dumbfounded. Why on earth had Karen told him what she had said? She had thought that they were becoming friends.

Still, she supposed that Karen thought herself to be in love, so her loyalty was to Gary.

'Penny for your thoughts,' David said. He had returned wearing a clean white shirt which showed off his tan beautifully.

Seeing him, Eve nearly forgot about Gary. Her new husband just looked so handsome.

'Oh, I wasn't thinking of anything in particular,' she replied, not wanting to admit Gary had confronted her. 'Haven't we seen some wonderful animals? Now, all we need is to see a rhino.'

'Yes, that would be fantastic,' David replied, completely unaware of what was really going through Eve's mind.

She felt guilty for hiding things from him, but she didn't want to tell him what Gary had said. David could easily become worried — especially after she had told him about Gary's apparent willingness to commit murder.

9

The following morning, Eve went down early for the game drive, wanting to grab a cup of strong black coffee before it started. She hadn't been able to sleep much and was feeling tired.

She had tossed and turned all night, thinking about Karen. Granted, she hardly knew the girl, but she liked her and didn't want her to get hurt. Eve was certain Gary was up to no good.

Then there was Lawrence Brady. If Gary hadn't killed him, who had? She felt that it must be someone in their group, and perhaps the rest of them were in danger as well.

Eve was frustrated. She was out of her depth and she didn't like the feeling at all.

She had left David in bed. Something had upset his stomach and he was feeling terrible. Eve had offered to give up the morning game drive to stay with him, but he had refused. He said he was much better off sleeping and there was no need for Eve to miss out on the fun.

Reluctantly, she agreed. She suddenly realised that she now preferred to share experiences with her husband. This feeling was new and surprising to her. She had never minded doing things on her own before she got married.

When Eve entered the restaurant, the only person she saw was Hamisi. Perhaps he was the killer — although he had sounded shocked when Gary had talked about getting rid of somebody.

However, there was something suspicious about him. Why was he following Gary everywhere? Perhaps Gary had some hold over him and he had to do what he was told.

The drive wasn't taking place until seven that morning, so Eve thought she might as well have some breakfast before rather than after.

Eve filled her plate with different bean dishes, eggs and fresh bread from the buffet. It all looked delicious and she was soon tucking in, although she felt a little guilty that David was missing out.

She chose to sit on the table next to Hamisi. She smiled at him and he smiled back.

'Are you going on a game drive today?' she asked him.

'Sort of,' he said. 'I am here to work.'

'Oh, what do you do?'

He hesitated. 'I take photos of the animals. To put in magazines and so on.'

'How exciting,' Eve replied. 'Do you know Gary, our tour guide? Perhaps you could come with us to see the animals?'

'I don't know him at all, I'm sorry.'

Eve said nothing. Obviously Hamisi had forgotten seeing her back at Taita Hills — or perhaps he was hoping she had forgotten him.

Things were getting interesting. Hamisi was lying through his teeth — and the more she thought about it, the more convinced she was that he could be the killer.

* * *

Eve found herself sitting behind Gary in the Jeep, with Karen next to her. Karen had insisted that Eve sat with her.

Eve decided not to mention the fact that Gary had confronted her. Karen seemed so cheerful, and Eve knew it was often difficult to find happiness in this world.

Karen, too, was wary of mentioning the previous evening. She knew Gary had spoken to Eve, but she didn't want anything to ruin her delight in having Gary back, and as Eve wasn't talking about it, why stir things up?

Gary sat in the seat at the front of the Jeep, next to Adhama. He turned often to speak to Karen and even included Eve in his conversation.

Eve wondered why. Had he forgiven her for what she had said to Karen, or was he just pretending to be nice as Karen liked her?

When they stopped near a pride of lions, another Jeep turned up and Eve noticed Hamisi was in it. He was busy taking photos. Perhaps he was genuine after all — or was this just a cover-up? Had he talked to Gary about her and had they planned this charade?

Eve wanted to share her thoughts with David on her return to the lodge, but she didn't want to upset him. He would think she was getting involved with matters which didn't concern her.

She decided to speak to Gary.

'That man over there with the flashy camera — he was with you at Taita Hills, wasn't he?'

'No,' Gary replied too quickly. 'I've never seen him before in my life.'

'Oh, I must be mistaken. He looks very similar.'

'Perhaps he has a double.' Gary laughed.

Eve smiled, but she was certain she

was right. She had a brilliant memory for faces.

*　　*　　*

When they got back to the lodge, Eve went straight to see how David was. Despite her mind being a mass of confusion, she wasn't going to tell him anything. He would only worry, or at the worst, he would be cross with her.

As she walked along the corridor towards their room, she saw Gary and Hamisi going into a room together. Approaching, she saw that the door had been left ajar. She almost smiled; they really weren't much good at shutting doors behind them. Anyone could eavesdrop, although she did have to strain to hear what they were saying.

'Gary, I'm worried about one of the women on your tour. She recognizes me from Taita Hills.'

'That's Eve Masters. She said the same to me, but I denied it. I hope you did too.'

'Yes, of course.'

'Better keep our distance for the moment.'

'OK, Boss.'

Eve was trembling. She was right. There was something going on between those two.

Worried that they might catch her, Eve made a dash for it.

Entering her room, she saw David sitting up.

'How are you, darling? You look a lot better.'

'I do feel much better. I skipped breakfast, but I might try something light for lunch. Hopefully I'll be up to the afternoon game drive.'

'I hope so too. It was great this morning.'

Eve was finding it difficult to act normally and she hoped David wouldn't notice. Gary and his friend were aware of her interest in them. She couldn't trust them one bit and was wondering if her life could be in danger.

* * *

When David and Eve sat down to lunch, Sophie asked if she could join them.

'Of course,' Eve replied, even though she didn't particularly care for her. She was quite surprised, as apart from the beginning of the holiday, Sophie and Richard had kept themselves to themselves.

'Where's Richard?' Eve asked.

'He's not too well. Stomach troubles.'

'Oh, David wasn't too good either this morning, but he is better now.'

Tears filled Sophie's eyes.

'What's wrong, Sophie?' David asked.

David was always very sensitive to the troubles of others, unlike Eve who was basically just nosey.

'I have to tell someone. Can I rely on your discretion?

'Of course,' Eve said, suddenly interested.

Sophie got a tissue out of her bag and

wiped her eyes gently, so as to not smudge her make-up.

'I think my husband may have killed Lawrence.'

Eve gasped, but then composed herself.

'Why should you think that?' she asked.

'Lawrence was an old boyfriend of mine. It was such a coincidence that he was on the same safari as us. Richard was very annoyed when he saw him here. He thought Lawrence had followed us, but that can't be possible. How on earth would he have known we were going on this particular safari? They had a blazing row at Taita Hills. Now they've eliminated Gary as the killer, it can only be Richard.'

Eve was dumbfounded. This certainly was a turn up for the books.

'Has Richard ever shown signs of aggression?' she asked.

'Not really, he's normally quite placid, but Lawrence really got his back up.'

'You haven't told the police?' Eve asked.

'Of course not. He's my husband and I love him. But I am scared. He did suggest that I told Lawrence that we were coming on this safari and that I invited him. I mean, that would have been a crazy thing to do. We could hardly have spent any time together with Richard around, could we?'

'And did you invite him?' Eve asked.

'Of course not. I was over him. I love Richard, but he doesn't seem to believe me. I have no idea how Lawrence knew I was on this holiday.'

'Perhaps you should tell the police,' Eve suggested. 'I mean, if Richard could kill one person, there's no guarantee that he won't kill again — and that person might be you.'

'No, I can't tell the police!' Sophie exclaimed. 'They'll probably arrest him with no evidence.'

'Why have you told us?' David asked, wishing that she hadn't. Eve was too interested.

'Because I can't bear it. Richard has been so different on this trip. You may be right that he wants to kill me.'

David and Eve looked at each other.

'You will have to tell the police if you're that scared,' Eve said gently.

'I can't.' Abruptly Sophie stood up and made a dash out of the restaurant.

'What did you make of that, David?' Eve asked.

'I don't know, but one thing I do know is that you are going to keep your nose out of it. If Richard is a crazed killer, you might not be safe.'

Eve nodded, but inside she knew she wouldn't be able to leave it alone. She couldn't believe it; she had two mysteries to unravel. What a honeymoon this was turning out to be.

10

After the game drive the following morning, Eve was in the little shop at the lodge looking for souvenirs when she saw Ken Ferguson chatting to Gary as they walked towards the front entrance.

Eve's curiosity was aroused, so she put down the T-shirt she was looking at and nipped out of the shop. As she reached the lodge entrance, she saw Gary and Ken getting into a Jeep.

Eve was very surprised. Where on earth were they going, and why wasn't Joan with them? Ken couldn't possibly be having a private game drive, could he?

Eve went back in to the lobby and saw Joan talking to Kate. This was her opportunity.

'Joan, where's your husband gone? I saw him getting into a Jeep with Gary.

There's nothing wrong is there?'

'Is it any of your business?' Joan retorted. 'You need to keep your nose out of our affairs.'

'There's no need to be so rude,' Eve replied.

With that, she turned and left. David hurried after her. He had been sitting in the lobby while she had been looking in the shop.

'What was all that about?' he asked.

'There's something fishy going on here. Gary is up to no good, I'm sure. I just saw him get in a Jeep with Ken.'

'Please, Eve, don't get involved,' David begged. 'We're having such a lovely honeymoon. Anyway, it's hardly likely that they're doing anything wrong.'

'I'm sorry, darling. I'm just a bit worried for Karen. She's fallen head over heels in love with Gary and I'm sure it will all end in tears.'

'It's nothing to do with us, Eve.'

Eve felt guilty. After her last adventure, she had promised David never to get involved in other people's business again, but she couldn't help it. She didn't like Gary and knew he had secrets.

She had to find out what he was up to — even if it meant keeping it from David again. He would be upset if he found out, but she didn't think he would leave her now — not so soon after their wedding.

★ ★ ★

Not feeling like sunbathing that morning, Eve decided to use the internet to check up on emails. While at the computer, she searched for information on Gary again. However, she discovered nothing new. She thought how clever he must be to hide what he was involved in. Then she tried Ken Ferguson, but again there was nothing untoward.

However, when she went over to her Facebook page, she decided to do a search for Gary and Ken on the networking site. Gary didn't seem to have an account, but Ken did. Eve was excited that she was having some luck at last — but what she saw was more than she had bargained for. Ken's cover picture was a shot of him holding on to a dead giraffe.

Eve felt sick. What was this man doing on a safari if all he wanted to do was shoot animals?

She also remembered that Joan had said this was their first safari, but they must have been in Africa before — at least, Ken had. They were out and out liars.

As Eve read Ken's posts, she realised this was something he had been doing for a while, in different parts of the world.

What if that was where he had been going with Gary? Could Gary be involved in hunting? Little as she liked him, he seemed to love the animals and was a great guide. Was it just an act?

Her anger started to build up. As well as killing animals that were on their way to extinction, Gary would be making a fortune with two businesses.

Eve didn't know what to do. It was possible to get licences for hunting, so it wasn't illegal. Yet could she bear to continue on safari with someone who wanted to kill such beautiful creatures?

Should she tell David? No — he'd want to know why she was still pursuing Gary.

Perhaps she should confront Gary herself? Yes, that was the best idea . . . or so Eve thought.

★   ★   ★

Ken and Gary were gone all day. The group met up in the late afternoon for another game drive, and Eve noticed that Joan was there alone. Eve went over to her.

'Is Ken not coming? I thought he loved the game drives. He's taken so many photos and seems enthralled by the animals.'

Joan glared, but answered politely enough.

'He is, but he's got a jippy stomach.'

'Really?' Eve said. 'You know that I saw him go off with Gary earlier today.'

'What are you insinuating? I don't know why he went with Gary, but I can assure you he's in bed now. Don't you believe me?'

Eve almost said no, but everyone would think that she was crazy — most of all David. He would want to know what was going on and she had resolved not to tell him.

'Yes, of course I believe you,' Eve lied, and waltzed off.

Joan obviously knew what her husband was up to, but didn't seem to want to partake in his activities. However, Eve didn't think that this made her much better than him.

A moment later, Adhama came in.

'I'm afraid that Gary won't be coming on this drive as he's been held up, so you just have me.'

No one seemed to mind, even Joan, who had complained loudly when Gary had been arrested and wasn't there to take a game drive. It was obvious she knew what her husband was up to.

Eve started to get angry again. It didn't matter if what they were doing was legal or not. Animals shouldn't be hunted, particularly for fun. Eve made up her mind that she couldn't let this rest.

Gary probably wouldn't go to jail, not if he had arranged all the hunts legally, but it might put lots of people off using his holiday company. It would be so satisfying to see him go out of business.

* * *

Eve and David came in late for dinner. Kate, seeing them, immediately waved them over.

'Why don't you join us? We've just come in. I think most people are already on their desserts.'

'Thank you, we'd love to,' Eve answered.

She was getting to like Kate and

James. Kate reminded her of Annie back on Crete. Both were sympathetic, kind women.

It was a buffet that evening and they all piled their plates high with the delicious food.

'I shall be putting on weight with all these fantastic dishes,' Kate remarked.

'It is all so good, isn't it?' Eve replied.

As they sat down, Eve glanced around the room. Gary was back and Karen was sitting with him, starry-eyed. Richard was sitting on his own, averting his eyes from everyone. Eve suspected that he and Sophie hadn't mended any fences.

Joyce had joined Joan and Ken, and Eve felt sorry for her. Joan was speaking loudly about her trip to India to see the tigers. Her admiration of the animals sounded genuine. How could she condone Ken's behaviour?

Eve felt her anger brimming again, but she tried to suppress it. David was very good at sensing her moods and she didn't want him to know that she planned to get involved in Gary's activities.

To put it out of her mind, she started talking about life on Crete.

'I can't believe you've been involved in so many murders and mysteries, Eve,' Kate exclaimed. 'It sounds so exciting. Perhaps you will be able to solve Lawrence's murder?'

'She will not,' David exclaimed, a little too harshly in Eve's opinion. 'I've lost count of how many times I thought I was going to lose you,' he said more softly, looking into Eve's eyes.

Eve took David's hand and smiled at him.

'I promised you that I wouldn't interfere,' Eve said gently, kissing him on the cheek. 'Let's order some more wine. We are on holiday after all.'

She felt guilty, but it was best that she didn't tell David about Gary and Ken. She wasn't really lying, after all; she was investigating Gary's hunting business, not the murder. It could of course all be connected to Lawrence and it might lead to trouble, but she couldn't help herself.

★ ★ ★

Everybody went to the bar after dinner except for Joyce, who excused herself and went to bed. Sophie, who had arrived late for dinner, seemed to be knocking her drinks back, and Eve couldn't help but think that she was hiding something.

Gary and Karen had been joined by Adhama, and Eve could see a look of frustration on Karen's face. She obviously wanted Gary to herself.

Their drinks were getting low and Eve was just about to ask David to go and get another round, when she saw Ken alone at the bar getting drinks for himself and Joan. Eve jumped up.

'I'll get the next round in. Stay and chat, David.'

When she got to the bar, Ken was just about to leave with his drinks.

'Feeling better, Ken?' she asked sweetly.

'What?' he replied.

'Joan said you were ill.'

'Oh — yes,' he said unconvincingly. 'I'm much better, thanks.'

Eve smiled. Ken hadn't been ill at all. She decided to throw caution to the wind, which wasn't too difficult after the wine and gin and tonics.

'I know where you've been, Ken. I saw you going off with Gary.'

'What do you mean?'

Eve noticed that he had started to perspire.

'You've been hunting. How could you? You pretend to love the animals, and then you go off and kill them.'

'Rubbish. Whatever gave you that idea?'

'I saw your Facebook page,' Eve said simply.

Ken looked very agitated. There was no way out. He had to admit it.

'So what if I have been hunting? It's all legal.'

'It might be legal, but it's not at all ethical.'

Ken paused for a moment.

'Well, it's nothing to do with you.'

With that he grabbed his drinks and left.

Eve felt a great sense of satisfaction. She had been right — but if it was legal, what could she do about it?

Eve ordered some drinks and decided that she was going to talk to Gary the next day.

11

Eve tossed and turned all night. She didn't know what to do. She couldn't bear to think of all these animals being killed, either by poachers or people like Ken Ferguson.

It had to stop. If she only managed to close down one hunting business, at least that would be something.

Eve had almost forgotten about Lawrence, but then the memory of how he looked lying in bed with his throat cut suddenly flashed through her mind. If he really had been a reporter, perhaps he had got wind of what Gary was up to and wanted to write a damning story about him. However, Gary had been released by the police so he had got away with it.

Of course there was always the possibility that he could be innocent — but then, who had killed Lawrence?

Could Richard really have been so jealous that he was driven to murder?

It was the early hours of the morning when Eve finally dropped off, but her sleep was interrupted by dreams of Gary chasing her through the bush, with Ken and Joan watching and laughing.

★   ★   ★

Luckily for Eve, there wasn't a game drive arranged for the following morning, so she slept in. She was woken up by a clatter in the bathroom. She sat up quickly, her heart beating fast.

'Sorry, Eve,' David said coming into the bedroom. I dropped something. I didn't want to wake you — you looked sound asleep.'

'Don't worry. I'm sure it's time to get up. I am feeling peckish.'

'You didn't sleep very well, did you, darling?'

'I'm sorry if I woke you during the night. I have no idea why I couldn't sleep.'

She was lying to David again and she didn't want to. She knew she should try and forget about Gary and his hunting business, as well as Lawrence's murder, but it was so difficult.

Eve sat there for a moment, wondering how she could keep her promise to David. Finally, not finding any answers, she got up, kissed her gorgeous husband, and went to get ready.

When they went in to breakfast, the only people there were Joan and Ken. They both averted their eyes when they saw Eve looking at them. David wished them good morning, but received only a mumbled response.

'Well, they certainly don't seem to like us, do they, Eve?' he said as they went to the buffet.

'I think it's mainly me, so don't worry about it.'

'What have you done now, Eve?'

He knew Eve and Joan didn't get on, but had Eve done something else to upset them?

'Nothing,' Eve replied a little too

quickly. 'Joan is just so like Betty and has been rude to me, so I'm afraid I've had to answer her back.'

David decided not to pursue the subject. Whatever was going on couldn't have anything to do with Lawrence's murder, could it? Eve had hardly mentioned Lawrence, so he was pretty certain she had put the episode out of her mind.

Gary and Karen came in and Eve wondered if they had spent the night together. All of a sudden she felt like confronting him. Karen would have her eyes opened to what he was up to. She loved animals almost as much as Eve did.

'Hi, Eve — David,' Karen shouted out.

She seemed so happy, and Eve couldn't bear to think how let down she would feel if she knew what the real Gary was like. Perhaps it was best to keep quiet for the time being. She sighed.

★ ★ ★

Eve went out to the pool after breakfast and chose a bed to sunbathe on, while David popped back to the room to get a book. Just as Eve was putting her towel on the bed, she saw a shadow next to her. Looking up, she saw Gary.

'Oh, good morning, Gary,' she said, trying to sound normal.

He looked grim, and Eve suddenly felt her heart beating very quickly.

'Ms Masters. You need to keep your nose out of my business.'

'What do you mean?' Eve tried to smile.

'You know what I mean. Ken told me everything.'

Eve was trembling, but there was no way she could hide what she thought about hunting.

'How can you run a hunting business while at the same time take people out to see and admire the animals?' she demanded.

'My hunts are legal, so there is nothing you can do about it.'

'Isn't there? I could destroy your

holiday business.'

'Just you try, Ms Masters, and you will regret it. Karen tells me you have been involved in murders on Crete. Well, this isn't Crete. It's much more dangerous.'

With that, he turned and left.

Eve watched him leave. She was still shaking. Where had all her bravado gone? Perhaps she should leave well alone.

However, she then thought about those poor animals and her fear left her. Gary didn't know who he was dealing with.

*   *   *

Eve and David were ready and waiting for the safari Jeep later that afternoon. Gary was already there talking to Joan and Ken. Eve wondered if they were discussing another hunt. She didn't think Ken had come to kill just one animal.

Mind you, she imagined hunting

licences cost a pretty penny. Joan was prone to go on about how expensive things were and getting her money's worth, so how could she approve of so much money being spent on Ken's hobby?

Judging by Joan's reactions to Eve's questions the previous day, Eve couldn't believe that she knew nothing about her husband's activities.

Gary glanced at Eve, but didn't acknowledge her. Eve felt a trickle of fear run down her spine. She remembered his words at Taita Hills. He was ready to kill — so if he thought she was a threat, what was stopping him from murdering her?

Nevertheless, Eve couldn't stop her pursuit of Gary. If he and Ken were to go out on a hunt again, she would love to follow them. Then she could take photos as proof of what they were doing. While Ken had his grinning face plastered all over Facebook with his dead quarry, Gary didn't, and she wanted to change that.

However, it was impossible. She was stuck in the Serengeti and there was no way she could wander out into the bush on her own.

It wasn't long before all the others arrived. Sophie had on her sunglasses, even though they were inside. Eve wondered if she had been crying again. She then saw Richard touch Sophie's arm, and was surprised to see her flinch.

Eve wondered whether they were still arguing over Lawrence, despite the fact that he was dead.

Ever since the first day, when Sophie and Richard had seemed happy, they had either sat in silence or argued. Lawrence was dead, so he couldn't come between them — or could he? They had only been married for a year, so shouldn't they be happy? Eve couldn't imagine being like that after a year of marriage to her lovely David.

Her thoughts were interrupted by Gary announcing that it was time to get going. She felt excited again in spite of herself; they were bound to see more animals, and she never tired of it.

The game drive was as thrilling as always, but Eve became intrigued by Sophie again. Although she had professed to be a little scared of the animals, she had looked at them on previous game drives and had even taken a few photos. Today she seemed to just stare at the seat in front of her, sunglasses still on, even though it was cloudy.

Her husband completely ignored her and focused on taking photos. Eve guessed they'd had another row.

As they arrived back at the lodge, everyone got up, satisfied after another successful game drive. Eve was especially pleased to see more cheetahs and was even impressed by the vultures. All thoughts about Gary and Lawrence had temporarily left her.

As she got off the bus, she was suddenly grabbed by Sophie who had missed the last step. She turned to help her and noticed that the first thing

Sophie did was grab her sunglasses, which had fallen off. However, Eve had glimpsed her black eye before she shoved them back on.

'Are you all right?' Eve asked gently, referring to her fall.

'Yes, yes, I'm fine,' Sophie said and quickly left, followed by Richard.

'Did you see that, David?' Eve asked.

'What?'

'Sophie had a black eye. Richard must have punched her. They've been arguing a lot in the last couple of days, don't you think?'

'Yes, I have noticed their arguments, but it's nothing to do with us. It's between them.'

'But David — he might kill her next time. She's such a tiny thing.'

'You can't tell the police here that, Eve. Remember how officious they were back at Taita Hills. They might falsely arrest Richard. And anyway, it's up to her to report him if he did really hit her. She could just have walked into a door.'

'Oh David, that's practically impossible. If you walk into a door, you are more likely to hit your head or a part of your body, not get a black eye.'

'Eve, please leave it alone. Our honeymoon has been great so far. Can't we keep it like this?'

'Fine. I'm just worried for Sophie, but I suppose you're right.'

Eve sighed. She could understand David's point of view, but if Sophie was a battered wife, somebody had to help her.

12

The following afternoon there was another game drive. Everybody turned up at four pm, including Sophie and Richard. She still had her sunglasses on.

The previous evening, Richard had come to dinner on his own. He had eaten very quickly and left, taking a plate of food with him, no doubt for Sophie. Well, Eve thought, she could hardly wear sunglasses at dinner.

This afternoon Joan and Ken asked if they could go to the hippo pool as they had missed it first time round. Nobody objected, even though Eve thought that the only reason Ken wanted to go was to size up the hippos for a future hunt.

When they stopped at the hippo pool, everybody got out of the Jeep so that they could view the animals from above. They were all very excited, even though it was the second visit for most of them. Eve watched Ken taking photos and felt angry again. Did he have no conscience?

A few minutes later, Eve noticed that Richard and David were talking. Sophie was standing all alone so Eve grabbed her chance.

'Sophie, I know you have a black eye. Did Richard do this to you?'

'No,' Sophie murmured. 'I walked into a door.'

'I don't believe you. If Richard is hurting you, you need to get away from him.'

'I told you it wasn't him. And even if it was, I couldn't very well go to the police here. They scared the living daylights out of me back at Lake Manyara.'

'Yes, you're right about that. I don't usually get fazed by the police, but I wasn't that keen on those two. However, you need to do something when you get home.'

Sophie said nothing, but wiped away

a few tears. Eve was lost as to what to do. Sophie was stuck here in Tanzania at the mercy of Richard. She just hoped he wouldn't hurt her again.

David turned and saw Eve standing next to Sophie. He frowned, hoping that his new wife hadn't been quizzing her.

Seeing David, Eve moved away from Sophie and walked towards him, hugging him.

'Aren't the hippos wonderful?' she said. 'It's great to have another opportunity to see them. It's a good job I charged my camera battery.'

'What were you saying to Sophie?' David asked, ignoring what she had said. 'I hope you didn't broach the subject of her black eye, Eve.'

'Of course not,' Eve lied. 'We were talking about the hippos.'

David looked at Eve, wanting to believe her, but as much as he tried, he couldn't. Even though she had promised that she wouldn't interfere in other people's affairs, he knew that she would find it very difficult.

He sighed. Eve would never change completely, but nevertheless, he couldn't help but love her.

* * *

As Eve and David walked into the lodge, they stopped. Right in front of them were the two police officers who had interviewed them when Lawrence had been found murdered.

Eve looked at David and he at her. The policemen were so officious that both felt guilty even though they had done nothing.

Everybody else started wandering in, and stopped when they saw the officers. Gary went to greet them. Eve thought he didn't look as assured as normal.

'Officers, are you here to see us? Have there been developments in Lawrence Brady's case?'

'Yes — we are here to arrest Richard Blair for the murder of Lawrence Brady.'

There were gasps and murmurs. Everyone turned to look at Richard. Sophie let out a scream.

Richard stared at the police officers — and then he was gone, out of the door and running.

Eve thought how crazy he was. How far did he think he would get out in the bush, especially with all the wild animals about?

Richard dashed outside and saw Adhama talking to another man. Glancing into the Jeep, he saw that the keys were still in the ignition. He jumped in, revved up and was gone in a flash, just as the officers came outside.

'Quick, let's follow him,' Abasi, the chief inspector, said to Bayana, his assistant. They jumped into their vehicle and sped off. The group had come outside and watched them leave.

Eve stood there open-mouthed. Had Richard really killed Lawrence after all, even though his relationship with Sophie had ended long ago? Or that was what Sophie had claimed.

Eve looked around and saw Sophie, still with her sunglasses on. She was standing all alone and Eve could tell she was trembling. Eve started to go towards her when David took her arm.

'Eve,' he said urgently. 'Don't get involved.'

'I'm sorry, David, but Sophie needs someone. I'll just talk to her, that's all.'

David took his arm away and nodded. He wasn't happy, but then Eve was just going to comfort Sophie, or so he hoped. Nobody else seemed to want to go near her.

'Sophie,' Eve said, not really knowing what to say. 'You look like you could do with a drink.'

Sophie nodded and Eve led her to the bar, David following. Everybody else seemed to be talking amongst themselves, even Gary.

Eve thought he should have come over to check on Sophie, but he was so entrenched in his conversation with Karen that it seemed he had forgotten that Richard had a wife.

Eve asked David to get them all brandies and led Sophie to an empty table.

'Don't you think you should take those glasses off, Sophie?' Eve said gently.

Sophie shook her head.

'OK, if you feel more comfortable with them on, but the police will expect you to take them off when they interview you.'

'The police!' Sophie exclaimed. 'What will they want with me? It's Richard they've accused.'

'Yes, but you're his wife. They will want to find out if you know anything.'

'I don't know anything at all,' she replied, almost in tears.

'Come on, Sophie. Richard knew about your relationship with Lawrence. Why would he kill him otherwise?'

'I don't believe any more that he killed Lawrence. I know I said I thought he had, but he's not capable of murder. Anyway, Lawrence and I ended our relationship when I met Richard.'

'Richard hit you, so he obviously has a temper.'

'That's not the same as killing someone.'

Sophie started crying again, just as David came back with the brandies. Eve was a bit annoyed that he had returned so soon. She was sure she could wheedle the truth out of Sophie if they were alone. With David there, she knew she had to behave herself.

'Here, Sophie, drink this,' David said. 'It will calm you down.'

She nodded and gulped the drink down. Then she started coughing loudly and Ken and Joan, who were standing at the bar, turned round. They looked at Sophie quickly and then looked away.

Then Gary came in and made a beeline for Sophie. He glared at Eve, then spoke to Sophie.

'Are you all right, Mrs Blair? I'm sure it's just a mistake. They arrested me and then let me go.'

Sophie stared at him. Gary felt a little

awkward. Even Eve wasn't speaking. He cleared his throat.

'The police will want to talk to you when they get back, so you will need to calm down.'

Eve butted in. 'How can she? Her husband's just been arrested.'

Gary glared at Eve again, but she didn't care. Then a thought crossed Eve's mind. Wasn't it strange that Sophie hadn't asked about her husband? He was being chased by the Tanzanian police and they were bound to have guns.

'What will happen to Richard when he's caught?' she asked. 'I would imagine that the police know the Serengeti better than Richard.'

Gary paused and Eve saw that he looked uncomfortable. Would he tell her the complete truth or would he try to flower it up?

'Well,' Gary said. 'They will bring him back for questioning. It's hardly likely he'll get away. I mean, he doesn't know the area round here.'

'They might shoot him,' Sophie said, with no emotion in her voice.

Eve and David looked at each other, but they were both thinking different things. David believed that Sophie was in a state of shock, while Eve thought that she simply didn't care what happened to her husband.

'I'm sure it won't come to that, Mrs Blair,' Gary said eventually. 'Why don't you go and lie down?'

'No, I'll wait here until Richard comes back dead or alive.'

With that, she downed the last of her brandy.

'I'm having another. Anyone joining me?'

13

Richard turned the key and shoved the Jeep into gear. The car made a sputtering sound but seconds later, it burst into life and he was off.

He looked in the mirror, but the police weren't behind him yet. He was sure they would follow him, but he had taken part in rallies and was used to rough terrain. If he kept following the track, it was sure to take him out of the Serengeti.

What he would do then, he didn't know. He just didn't want to be arrested. He thought the police might be ruthless and wouldn't give him a chance to prove his innocence.

He had his mobile in his pocket. Perhaps he could ring Sophie later and arrange to meet her after the safari. He had money and credit cards, so they could hide out in some obscure hotel.

He didn't consider the fact that the police would have his credit cards traced or that they could inform the airport and border controls so that he would be stopped if he tried to leave the country.

Richard looked in the mirror again and there was a vehicle in the distance. Was it the police? He couldn't take a chance. He put his foot on the accelerator.

Richard was beginning to regret his decision to flee. What was he thinking of? He told himself he was innocent, so what could the police do? However, they might not believe him. Then what? He would be thrown into some grotty jail where he would rot away. He had to take his chance.

He wasn't concentrating properly and suddenly he saw an elephant in front of him. He swerved, his heart beating nineteen to the dozen, but he managed to just avoid the startled animal and get back on the track.

Richard was trembling and became

fully aware of where he was and what a foolish thing he was doing. What if he did get away from the police? He could still break down and not get out of the Serengeti alive.

It was getting dark and he felt truly scared for the first time. What had got into him? This just made him look guilty. He hadn't thought it out. All he knew was that he didn't want to face interrogation, but it was stupid. If the police caught him now, they would probably throw him into jail immediately, or maybe even shoot him.

He was in a strange country and he had no idea how corrupt the police were. They might be under orders to close the case as soon as possible. Perhaps they didn't care if he was innocent or not. They could just want someone to blame.

★   ★   ★

Back at the lodge, Sophie had finished her third brandy and even taken off her sunglasses. A few of the others had stared at her black eye, but no one was brave enough to ask her about it.

'Anyone want another drink?' Sophie asked.

'No thanks,' Eve said. 'Don't you think you should eat something before having another? The restaurant will be open by now. We'll go in with you.'

'I'm not hungry,' Sophie snapped and got up, heading for the bar.

'What are we going to do with her?' Eve asked David. 'She's going to be blotto soon. What if the police come back with Richard and want to talk to her? They'll be lucky to find her coherent.'

'There's nothing we can do, Eve. She's a grown woman.'

Eve sighed. She wished she hadn't suggested a drink to Sophie, but she had no idea that this would happen.

Kate, seeing Sophie at the bar, popped over to talk to Eve and David.

'How's Sophie taking this? We didn't want to intrude.'

'Well, she's not said much,' Eve replied. 'However, she's drinking too much. We don't know what to do.'

'Kate,' Sophie said jovially, coming back with a fourth large brandy. 'Why don't you join us? We can talk about my murderous husband. How could he do that to poor Lawrence? He was such a lovely man. Would make any woman happy.'

'Did you know Lawrence before you came on this trip?' Kate asked, looking astounded.

Eve wished that Sophie would shut up. She was beginning to make a case for Richard killing Lawrence.

'Did I know Lawrence?' Sophie laughed drunkenly. 'I was going to marry him before Richard came along and stole me away.' She giggled. 'Lawrence was such a *lovely* man . . . '

With this, Sophie collapsed on the floor, her glass breaking to smithereens.

★　★　★

Richard was still managing to keep the police at bay, but he was starting to panic. It was dark now; it had come on suddenly and he wasn't even sure if he was still on the track. Was he even travelling in the right direction? However, he feared that if the police caught up with him now, they would shoot him.

He pressed his foot down, but the Jeep wouldn't go any faster. All of a sudden an animal ran in front of him. He wondered stupidly what it was. He swerved and missed it, but before he could regain control the Jeep careered into a tree. In his rush to escape, he hadn't put a seat belt on.

A couple of minutes later, the police officers stopped behind the crashed vehicle. They jumped out, holding guns, but soon put them away when they saw Richard slumped over the steering wheel.

'Is he dead?' Bayana asked.

Abasi felt his pulse.

'No, he's alive, but his face is a mess.

He must have smashed it on the windscreen.'

Richard started to stir, moaning with pain. The two officers took their guns out again.

'Get out of the Jeep.' Abasi spoke sharply.

Richard struggled to obey, but as he put his left leg on the ground, he screamed.

'I think my leg is broken.'

The two officers looked at each other, not knowing whether to believe him. Richard tried to put weight on his leg again, but still couldn't.

'Better put him in our Jeep and get him to the hospital,' Abasi said. 'He will have to have an armed guard.'

'An armed guard?' Richard exclaimed. 'My leg is probably broken. How am I going to run away?'

The officers didn't answer, but started dragging Richard to their Jeep. They settled him in the back and Bayana sat next to him, holding his gun.

'Why did you run from us?' Abasi

asked. 'Don't you know that it makes you look guilty?'

'I have no comment. I want a lawyer.'

'Very well. You will have one when we get to Dar es Salaam.'

Richard closed his eyes. Things looked bad and it was all the fault of that woman he'd had the misfortune to marry. She had been nothing but trouble since they first met.

* ★ *

Sophie was sitting up after having passed out for a good ten minutes. Eve had fetched her a large glass of water. She was desperate to ask Sophie more about her and Lawrence, but even she realised it wasn't the right time.

'Are you feeling better?' she asked instead.

'I think so. I wish everybody would stop staring at me though.'

The others had all gathered around.

'We are all just concerned about you,'

Eve assured her. 'I'm sure this has been a shock.'

Sophie nodded.

'I really just want to lie down,' Sophie said, 'but I am so worried about Richard. Those police officers might have shot him.'

Suddenly she burst into tears. Eve was surprised that she was now worried about Richard, when she had been so concerned about Lawrence a few minutes previously. Sophie was obviously in a state of shock.

'I'm pretty sure the police won't have shot your husband, Sophie,' Gary said. 'Not unless he points a gun at them. I presume he hasn't got any weapons?'

'Of course not,' snapped Sophie. 'How on earth would he have got anything like that through customs?'

She took another sip of water.

'I think we should all go and eat, while waiting to hear what has happened.' Gary said. 'Time is getting on.'

Everybody agreed and they all piled into the dining room, apart from

Sophie and Eve.

'I don't think I can eat anything,' Sophie said.

'Try just a little. You'll need to keep your strength up.'

'What for? For when the police interrogate me?' Sophie said, shivering.

'They're bound to want to talk to you, Sophie, but I'm sure they won't give you a hard time,' Eve said, not entirely convincingly. She took Sophie's arm and led her to the restaurant.

Gary suggested that they all sat together, and once they had chosen a seat, they went and helped themselves to the buffet. The mood was sombre and nobody said a lot, not even Eve.

About half way through the meal, Gary's phone rang. He answered it and all the others could hear him speaking. All he seemed to say was yes and no. When he closed the call, he walked over to Sophie, who was looking as white as a sheet.

'Sophie, the police have Richard, but he crashed the Jeep and is being taken to hospital in Dar es Salaam.'

'Oh my God,' Sophie exclaimed. 'What's happened to him? Is he badly hurt?'

'It sounds as if he could have a broken leg.'

'He's such an idiot. I don't know why he ran from the police. It was obvious he could never get away — not out here. Anyway, I'm sure he didn't kill Lawrence. He's not a murderer.'

Sophie burst into tears again and Eve put her arm around her to comfort her.

'The police want to question you, so they will be back tomorrow. I'm sorry if that frightens you, but that's what they said.'

'What about the safari?' Eve asked. 'The Jeep is out of use, I presume?'

Joan, sitting close by, was listening intently.

'I will arrange for another Jeep, but we probably won't be able to go out in the bush tomorrow.'

'Well, really,' Joan piped up. 'This holiday is being ruined. Ken and I were looking forward to this trip so much. I shall complain, of course.'

Eve wanted to ask if they had been looking forward to the holiday so that Ken could shoot animals, but decided to keep quiet.

'I'm sorry, Mrs Ferguson,' Gary said, 'but this is out of my control. The itinerary will resume as soon as possible.'

'Does your partner know about this? I doubt if he'd be pleased to have dissatisfied customers.'

'I think he will be realistic and understand the situation,' Gary said calmly.

'I just want to go to bed,' Sophie interrupted. 'I feel shattered. I just hope I don't have nightmares.'

'OK,' Eve said. 'Do you want any help?'

'No, I'll be fine. Thank you for being so kind.'

Eve smiled and squeezed her hand.

When she had gone, David moved next to Eve.

'I'm proud of you not trying to solve this case yourself,' he said softly.

Eve smiled, but felt herself going red. He knew nothing about her encounter with Gary — nor did he know that as soon as she had a moment alone, she would search for information on Sophie and Richard.

14

The following morning, Eve was up early yet again. She hadn't had a lot of sleep and when she did finally drop off, she had a nightmare in which Gary chased her through the bush wielding a gun. Then later she dreamed that David left her because she hadn't told him that Ken was a hunter, nor about her confrontation with Gary.

Eve awoke, perspiring, at about half past five. She lay for a while trying to get back to sleep. David was sleeping soundly by her side and the old saying crossed her mind that the righteous always slept well.

Eventually, Eve got up quietly so as not to wake David, and went and sat in the bathroom with her laptop, deciding that there was no time like the present to look up Sophie and Richard. Why not take another look at

Lawrence as well?

Eve had already found out that Lawrence had been a reporter, but now she discovered that he had supported animal rights and often reported animal abuse cases.

Eve was astounded. How could she have missed this bit of information the last time she had searched the internet? It gave Gary the perfect motive to kill Lawrence. Eve was sure he wouldn't have wanted any negative publicity.

The police had let Gary go, but that didn't mean they had ruled him out completely. It was possible that they didn't have enough evidence to convict him.

However, why had Richard run from the police? Perhaps he had just been scared, but on the other hand he could be guilty.

In addition, Ken was a suspect. Much as he loved hunting, he wouldn't want to be in a national newspaper. There were so many people like herself who hated hunting, and he might have thought that he could be victimised.

Eve was getting excited and kept searching. She was almost ready to give up when she came across a surprising piece of news. It was only a fragment of information on a society gossip blog, but she was sure it was relevant.

Sophie had been just about to marry Lawrence, but she had left him literally at the altar to run off with rich socialite Richard Blair. Eve hadn't realised how serious Sophie's relationship with Lawrence had been.

However, wouldn't this have given Lawrence a motive to kill Richard, not the other way around? After all, Richard had got the girl.

Eve sat there thinking, her brain working overtime. Perhaps Lawrence had started pursuing Sophie, despite her marriage to Richard. Perhaps she wanted him back and told him all about this holiday — although Eve didn't know what good it would have done with Richard around.

Maybe Sophie had started seeing Lawrence again behind her husband's back. It seemed the only way he could have found out that she was going on this safari.

On the other hand, Lawrence could have been pursuing Gary with the hope of getting a good story. It might sound far-fetched, but perhaps it had been simply a coincidence that he had ended up on the same safari as Sophie and Richard.

The possibilities were endless, but she still had no idea who really was the killer.

Eve felt she couldn't just sit there and do nothing. She had to speak to Sophie.

Quickly she dressed and put on some make-up. Eve hated being seen looking anything but perfect, even this early in the morning. As she left the room, she checked to see if David was still asleep. Luckily for her, he was.

⋆   ⋆   ⋆

Sophie and Richard's room was only a couple of doors away and Eve just had to knock once.

'Who is it?' Sophie asked from behind the door, her voice trembling.

'It's me, Eve, open up.'

When Sophie opened the door, Eve's first thought was how tired she looked.

'Have you slept at all?' Eve asked.

'Not much. What do you want?' she asked, a little too sharply.

Eve ignored Sophie's tone, thinking that there was no reason to beat about the bush.

'I know that you and Lawrence didn't just have a fling. You left him on your wedding day for Richard.'

Sophie just stared at Eve for a moment.

'How did you find out?' she asked, her voice shaking.

'I did an internet search on all three of you.'

'Why would you do that?' asked Sophie, sounding shocked.

'I couldn't sleep thinking about the

whole situation. However, now things make even less sense. Lawrence had far more of a motive to kill Richard than the other way round — unless you told Richard you wanted to go back to Lawrence.'

Sophie said nothing, which worried Eve. Perhaps she had wanted to leave her husband for Lawrence after all.

'You know that you'll have to tell the police, don't you?' she asked instead. 'Mind you, they might already have found out about your connection with Lawrence. I came across the article easily enough. This could be why the police arrested your husband.'

Sophie dropped her head into her hands.

'OK, Eve, I'll tell you everything that happened. I don't think there's any point hiding my story from you. You've already got the gist of it. Plus it's tearing me apart keeping it all to myself.

'I tried to split up with Lawrence when I met Richard, but he took it so badly that I agreed to stay with him. However, when it came to our wedding day, I couldn't go through with it.

'I loved Richard, you see, or so I thought. We had a whirlwind romance, but a few months after our wedding, I realised what he was really like. Richard has a temper — though he hadn't ever hit me before, not until this black eye.

'A few weeks ago I agreed to meet Lawrence, and yes, we did have a short affair. He was so much nicer and kinder to me than Richard. One day he came to my house when Richard was away. He saw the tickets for this trip and was furious. He thought I was trying to make a go of my marriage to Richard.

'He stormed out and I didn't see him again until we came here. I ignored him and he ignored me, but Richard was livid. He didn't know about the affair, but he still thought that I had invited Lawrence on the trip.

'I hadn't, though.' Sophie paused. 'Now what do I do? Do I tell the police the truth or not? It'll condemn Richard.'

Sophie looked as if she was in total despair. Eve put a reassuring arm around her.

'I don't think you can do anything else apart from tell the police the truth. They must have found out that you were engaged to Lawrence at one time. I did, and it didn't take me long. Lawrence was quite famous as a reporter. Your engagement to him was probably the reason why they arrested Richard.'

'Oh Eve, you're probably right — but I don't know if I can send Richard to prison.'

'Richard has hit you. He probably won't stop now he's done it once. Better if he is in prison.'

'But we don't know if Richard really did kill Lawrence. It wouldn't be fair to put him in jail if he is innocent.'

Sophie burst into tears and Eve gave her a hug.

Did Sophie still love Richard after all

that had happened? she wondered. The girl had admitted to an affair with Lawrence after their marriage, so she couldn't have loved him that much . . . or perhaps that had been a mistake as well. Sophie really didn't seem to know what she wanted.

'Come on, let's get you some breakfast. You can't hide away in here.'

'I don't know if I can eat anything.'

'You'll need some strength to face the day ahead. You hardly ate anything yesterday. The police are bound to be back. And that's another thing — they might want you to go to Dar es Salaam with them.'

'Oh no!' Sophie wailed. 'I can't do that. I'll be all alone in a foreign city. Richard will probably be in hospital in police custody. No, I can't do it.'

'Well, if the police get all the information they want, they'll probably let you stay here,' Eve said, trying to calm Sophie down. 'After all, you haven't done anything wrong.'

Sophie wiped the tears away.

'Thank you for helping me. I was cracking up, but now I feel a little better.'

Eve smiled, but inside she was more than a little worried about what David would think. Granted, she wasn't out chasing killers — but she was getting involved in a murder investigation.

She'd have to prove she was simply supporting Sophie. It wouldn't be so difficult, would it?

* * *

Eve and Sophie were tucking into their breakfast when David came into the restaurant.

'There you are, Eve,' he said, sounding relieved. 'I was so worried when I woke up and found you weren't in our room. I quickly got up and dressed, but I haven't even shaved.'

'I'm so sorry, darling,' Eve said, getting up and kissing him on his rather stubbly cheek. 'I couldn't sleep for worrying about Sophie, so I got up and went to see her. You were sound asleep and I didn't want to disturb you. I should have left you a note. Will you forgive me?'

Showing surprising tactfulness, Sophie got up.

'I'm going to get some more fruit. I'm suddenly feeling hungry.'

'Oh Eve,' David said. 'Why do you always have to get involved with other people's business?'

'I'm only giving Sophie some support. She feels all alone here. The police have already got the culprit so there's not a lot I can do, is there?'

'I suppose not, if Richard really is guilty,' he said, cheering up a little. He cupped Eve's face in his hands and kissed her.

'Really, you should leave all that in the bedroom,' Joan said crossly as she walked by.

Eve just laughed. That woman truly needed to lighten up.

'I'm going to get some breakfast,' David said, completely ignoring Joan.

When David had gone, Sophie came back.

'Do you want me to leave you in peace with David?' she asked.

'No, don't be silly. Sit down. I'm pleased you've got your appetite back.'

Kate and James came in and asked to join them. Eve looked at Sophie who nodded.

'Honestly, I feel better with people around me. I'm so worried about being interviewed again.'

She hadn't mentioned Richard since her private revelations to Eve.

David came back with a plate piled high with delicious-smelling food.

'That lot could feed an army,' Eve commented.

'It probably could, but I'm starving and it will just about feed me.'

They all started to eat and the conversation turned to the animals they had seen. After exhausting that topic, silence fell like a dead weight. They all knew Sophie was nervous, but they didn't want to speak about the situation.

'I think I'll go and get a bath,' Sophie said, relieving the tension, 'before the police get here.'

'Good idea,' Eve replied.

Once she had gone, they all relaxed.

'I was reading some info about Lawrence Brady on the internet,' Kate remarked. 'It seems he's upset a lot of different people with his stories.'

'Really?' Eve replied. 'I thought he was mainly involved in exposing cases of animal cruelty.'

'Recently he was, but when he was younger, he reported scandals of the rich and famous.'

'That's very interesting,' Eve replied, wondering how she could have missed this.

David looked at her suspiciously.

'Have you been researching him, Eve?'

'Only a little. I was just interested.'

David was about to say something when all eyes turned to the door. The police had returned.

15

Sophie sat in front of the police officers. She didn't feel at all well. She had come over all hot and cold and she knew that she was perspiring.

Her hands were shaking and she couldn't do anything to stop the trembling. What would the two men ask her? Would they try to intimidate her? And, most important, would they ask about her black eye? It had gone down a little, but there were still obvious signs of bruising.

However, both men smiled at Sophie, and she felt a sense of relief. They didn't seem half as intimidating as in her previous interview.

'I don't think I introduced myself the other day,' one of the officers said. 'My name is Abasi, and I am in charge of this case. My associate is Bayana. We understand that this must be difficult for you.'

'How is my husband? I know he had an accident.'

'He has cuts and bruises and a broken leg. He will have to stay in the hospital for some time.'

Sophie nodded.

'I take it you knew Mr Brady, Mrs Blair?'

Sophie paused. How much should she tell them? How much did they already know? She decided to be as brief as possible before admitting to anything else.

'We were in a relationship until I met Richard. I left Lawrence for my husband.'

She decided not to tell them about her recent affair with Lawrence; not unless they asked.

'Did you know that Mr Brady was coming on this holiday?'

'No,' Sophie said. 'It was a complete shock to me. I have no idea how Lawrence found out that we were going on this safari.'

So far so good.

'I would imagine that your husband was jealous when he saw Mr Brady here?'

'No, he was angry. At first he thought it was a coincidence, but then he began to think that I'd told Lawrence where we were going on holiday.'

'And had you?'

'Why should I? I was happy with my husband.'

Sophie was feeling bolder and thought she could get away with some half-truths.

'And your black eye?' Abasi asked.

'I walked into a door,' Sophie answered a little too quickly.

'Don't lie to us,' Abasi said more sharply.

Sophie was suddenly scared again. Although she had calmed down, now they were asking more personal questions. If she told them Richard had hit her, he could be condemned without any more information.

However, what if they had somehow

found out about the recent affair she'd had with Lawrence? She didn't know how they could have, but nothing would surprise her.

Better to tell the truth about her eye. She didn't want to be named as an accessory to murder.

'OK, officer. Richard hit me. He has a bit of a temper.'

'Thank you, Mrs Blair, for being honest,' Abasi said. 'What was the reason for him hitting you?'

'Well, I was upset that Lawrence had been murdered. I didn't love him any more, but I still liked him. He didn't deserve to die such a horrible death. Richard didn't think that I should have any feelings at all for Lawrence.'

'I see,' Abasi said, which Sophie thought could mean anything.

'What happens to my husband now?' she asked, hoping to divert the conversation away from Lawrence.

'He will be questioned, but it seems like an open and shut case.'

Sophie felt sick again. Was Richard

really going to jail for murder? Had she accelerated this process? Guilt overwhelmed her. Despite everything, she still had feelings for Richard.

'But there's no real evidence that Richard killed Lawrence,' she ventured.

'Really, Mrs Blair? I think we have evidence enough. You may go now.'

Sophie was upset by their abrupt dismissal of her. She got up to go, but her legs buckled under her. Both Abasi and Bayana jumped up to help.

'Are you all right, Mrs Blair?' Bayana asked.

'I think so. It's just the shock of all this. I would never have thought that my husband could have murdered anyone.'

Neither Abasi nor Bayana said anything, but helped Sophie to the door.

* * *

Eve was waiting when Sophie came out from her interview.

'So, how was it?' she asked as soon as they were round a corner and out of earshot, trying to keep the excitement from her voice. 'Did you tell them everything?'

She was desperate to know what had gone on in the interview.

'I told them most things, except that I'd had an affair recently with Lawrence. I didn't want them thinking I was a terrible person. I'm not, Eve, I'm just a bit weak. Lawrence kept pressurising me and in the end I gave in.'

'We can all act out of character sometimes,' Eve said diplomatically. 'But Sophie, if Richard had known about the affair, that could be further proof that he killed Lawrence. Or don't you want him convicted?

'Yes — no — I don't know.'

'You don't still love him, do you?'

'Yes, a bit, although it's been hard the way he's been recently. The first few months were idyllic, but he's such a possessive man. He was imagining all sorts of things. However, I do think he would have confronted me if he had suspected that I was having an affair with Lawrence.'

'One thing to hold on to is that the evidence is only circumstantial, Sophie. No one has come forward to say that they saw Richard entering Lawrence's room, have they? Nor have they found the weapon. However, I suppose things may be different here.'

Sophie shivered.

'I don't want him convicted if he hasn't done anything.'

'Well, who else could it be?' Eve asked, knowing full well that it could easily be Gary.

Eve was a little confused by Sophie. Sometimes she seemed to want to get rid of a husband who didn't seem to think twice about hitting her, and at other moments she felt sorry for him and was still even a little in love with him.

Gary appeared with most of the others from the group.

'Ladies — meeting on the patio.'

'I'll just go and get David,' Eve said. 'He's in our room.'

'How was the interview?' Kate asked Sophie.

'It wasn't too bad, Kate. The police were much more pleasant than last time.'

'No doubt they were aware that all this has come as a shock to you.'

Sophie nodded as she sat down, but said nothing else.

It wasn't long before Eve and David joined the group.

'Well, now that we're all here, we'll get started,' Gary said. 'I have arranged for a new Jeep, but I doubt it will be here in time for a game drive this afternoon.'

'Well, really, this is quite unsatisfactory — ' Joan boomed.

'If you'll let me finish, Mrs Ferguson. They have a small Jeep here so we can take you out in that in two groups. The game drive will be a little shorter, but at least you'll have a drive.'

'Humph. I still intend to complain.'

'You already have, Mrs Ferguson,' Gary said dismissively. 'So now, if you just want to have a leisurely day by the pool, I'll leave you to it. Perhaps you can decide on the groups between yourselves.'

As Gary left, Eve spoke.

'How about if David and I go with Kate, James, and Sophie?'

'Who put you in charge?' Joan spoke sharply.

'Well, I'm sure you don't want to come with me, do you?'

Joan glared at her, but said nothing.

'Karen, will you be all right going with Joyce, Joan and Ken?' Eve asked.

'Don't mind.' Karen spoke dreamily.

Eve shook her head. That girl was getting more and more obsessed with Gary. She felt like telling her what he was up to, but she had to admit she was worried about how Gary would react if she did. He had threatened her — and adding that to what she had overheard him say to Hamisi, she had no doubt that he would follow through.

*   *   *

David and Eve went to the pool to relax and sunbathe, but Eve was finding it hard to stop thinking about Sophie and Richard. Gary was also on her mind, as was Karen.

Eve now felt that she should go and tell the police about Gary and his threats, but they would want to know why she hadn't told them earlier. They may have been nice to Sophie, but there was no guarantee that they would be to her. No, it would probably be better if she kept quiet and didn't cause more problems for herself.

For the first time since they had left home, she wished that the honeymoon was over and she was back on Crete where she felt in control. She had conveniently forgotten about all the murders she had been involved in there, not to mention all her lucky escapes from death.

Eve was absorbed in her thoughts when the peace was interrupted by a scream from Joan and Ken's room. It was right by the pool so it couldn't be missed. Gary, who was sunbathing with Karen, jumped up. Joan came rushing out of her room through the French windows.

'Somebody has smeared *Murderer* all over our walls. We didn't even know Lawrence Brady.'

She was almost in tears, which surprised Eve. She thought that Joan was as tough as old boots.

'Calm down, Mrs Ferguson,' Gary said. 'Let's have a look at the damage.'

He walked over to their room, where Ken sat with his head in his hands. The room was a mess — and it wasn't just the writing on the walls. Their clothes and personal possessions were strewn all over the floor.

'Who could have done this?' Joan asked. All the colour had drained from her face.

'I don't know, but I think the police are still here, so I shall see if I can catch them.'

As Gary went to find Abasi and Bayana, everyone else came in and commiserated with them. Joyce even put her arm around Joan.

Eve was silent. Was the perpetrator actually accusing them of murdering Lawrence — or was it someone who had found out that Ken was a hunter and didn't like it? The second option seemed more likely, and for one brief moment Eve wished she'd had the courage to paint on their walls. It was what Ken deserved, after all.

★ ★ ★

The police hadn't left the lodge and it wasn't long before they went into Joan and Ken's room. Gary was with them. They looked sternly at the assembled group and told them to leave, which they all reluctantly did. Each of them wanted to know what was going on.

Kate, James, Eve, David and Sophie all went to sit together.

'Who on earth could have done such a terrible thing?' Kate asked. 'I can't believe that either Ken or Joan murdered Lawrence. I mean, they didn't even know him, did they?'

'I'm pretty sure they had never seen Lawrence before this trip,' Sophie said. 'Why should either of them want to kill him?'

'Perhaps it's all to do with something else, not Lawrence's murder,' Eve said.

'Like what, darling?' David responded. 'Nobody else has been murdered.'

Eve so wanted to tell the others that Ken was a hunter, but she kept her mouth shut. David would want to know how she knew, and then it would all come out, including Gary's threats.

A few minutes later, the police came out, followed by Joan and Ken. Joan looked as if she'd been crying. Eve tried to feel sorry for her, but she couldn't. Joan was a nasty piece of work and her husband was even worse.

Abasi spoke to the crowd.

'We will need to speak to all of you

individually. We will start with Eve Masters.'

Eve's heart started beating fast. Why was she first? Did they suspect she knew something, or think she was the one who had vandalised the room?

Eve got up reluctantly and followed Abasi and Bayana. As soon as she had sat down with them, Abasi spoke.

'What can you tell us about this latest development?'

'Me? Nothing. Why should I know anything?'

'Come on, Mrs Masters. You know that Mr Ferguson is a hunter. We've been told that you are involved with animal rights.'

'No, I'm not. I just don't think that animals should be killed, either for food or for fun. Anyway, who told you this?'

'Never mind who told us,' Abasi said.

It made no difference to Eve that they refused to tell her who the informant was. She knew it could only be Gary. He wanted her to be charged with this vandalism; she was sure of that.

The room went quiet. The police officers seemed to be waiting for Eve to say more. Finally she felt she had no choice but to tell them the truth.

'All right. I did find out that Ken was a hunter. I suppose that Gary told you.'

The two men waited for her to continue.

'Gary threatened me, you know. He told me to keep my nose out of his business.'

'But instead you vandalised the Fergusons' room.'

'No, I didn't. I'm not that stupid.'

Eve was becoming frustrated and a little scared. They were trying to pin this on her.

'Anyway, I couldn't have done it. I was with Sophie from early in the morning today. Ask her.'

'Don't think that we won't, Mrs Masters.'

Eve felt like telling them that she was Ms Masters, but thought it was probably the wrong time to assert her independence.

'Anyway,' Eve said, getting her confidence back. 'How do you know this was all about Ken and his hunting activities? Whoever vandalised the room could have been accusing either Joan or Ken of murdering Lawrence.'

'Yes, that is also a possibility,' Abasi agreed. 'We are looking at all options. I think that is all for now, Mrs Masters, Just don't leave the Serengeti for the time being.'

Eve was becoming angry. She got up abruptly.

'Where would I go? Out into the bush to be eaten by a leopard?'

The police officers just stared at her, so she decided it was time to leave.

'Send in Mr Thompson next, if you would, Mrs Masters.'

Eve was fuming, but left without saying anything else. They might arrest her for simply being rude!

She returned to the poolside and told James he was next.

'You were a while,' David observed. 'Is everything all right?'

'I'll tell you when all the interviews are done.'

Eve looked towards Gary, but he seemed to be deliberately avoiding her stare. *And so he should*, Eve thought. He had tried to get her arrested. It just wasn't on. This was her honeymoon and it was being ruined.

★ ★ ★

After the interviews, David and Eve went to their room. The other interviews hadn't taken long, certainly not as long as Eve's. She thought they might keep Sophie longer, but she said they asked very few questions. They wanted to know if she knew the Fergusons, and after answering in the negative, she had corroborated Eve's story that they had been together from early in the morning. Eve was now hopeful that the police wouldn't consider her a suspect.

As David went to sit down, Eve spoke to him.

'David, I have something to tell you.'

'Oh no, that sounds ominous. You haven't got embroiled in the murder case, have you?'

'No, of course not. I promised you I wouldn't get involved in any more murders, didn't I?'

'Yes, but you have promised me at other times and broken those promises.'

Eve suddenly felt annoyed. She was almost innocent this time. Would David never believe her? She took a deep breath and calmed down.

'It's nothing to do with Lawrence. It's about Ken Ferguson. Don't ask me any details, but basically I found out that he is a hunter and that Gary took him out one day to kill some poor innocent animals. Gary warned me not to get involved. He said that the hunts were legal, but obviously he doesn't want anyone to know as it might ruin his safari holiday business.'

'How dare he threaten you,' David said angrily, all thoughts of reprimanding Eve disappearing.

'That's not all, David. When we were at Taita Hills I heard him talk to somebody, a man called Hamisi. He keeps popping up wherever we are. When I overheard their conversation, Gary was threatening to get rid of somebody if they didn't do what he said. I have no idea who he wanted out of the way. I expect it was probably someone who works for him. Gary doesn't know I overheard him. At least I don't think so. Anyway, he must have told the police that I knew Ken was a hunter. He wanted to frame me for the vandalism.'

'That Gary needs a good talking-to. I know you have a tendency to interfere, but I won't stand for him threatening you.' David's eyes flashed.

Eve threw her arms around him.

'Oh darling, you're not cross with me then?'

'Not this time. I am angry about

Gary though. I m going to speak to him tonight.'

'No,' Eve said sharply. 'He's already got me into trouble with the police. They obviously know about his hunting business, so it must be legal, not that it makes it right.'

'OK, darling, but if the police start harassing you again, Gary won't know what's hit him.'

Eve looked at David. He hadn't told her off for once and he wanted to protect her. She really was lucky to have him as her husband.

* * *

Eve, David, Karen, James and Sophie were the first of the two groups to go on the game drive later that afternoon. There was one person missing, and that was Gary.

Eve thought that he was probably avoiding her and she couldn't blame him. She was pretty angry with him. She could have been arrested and thrown into some awful prison cell for something she hadn't done!

She had already decided to have a word with him herself. She didn't want to seem weak, and that's what she would look like if David went and talked to him. She had quickly forgotten how happy she had been when David had said he wanted to protect her.

'You just have me for the game drive today,' Adhama said with an apologetic shrug.

They all seemed happy with this, so Adhama started the Jeep and they were off.

Kate turned and spoke to Sophie.

'Did the police not suggest that you go to Dar es Salaam to see your husband?'

'No, they didn't mention it. I suppose I could have asked, but to tell the truth, I don't know if I want to see him.'

'You don't?' Kate exclaimed. 'Do you really think that he killed Lawrence?'

'I honestly don't know. Whatever, I

don't want to be in a city here on my own, which I would be. I hate staying in hotels alone. I feel so embarrassed if I have to eat on my own.'

'I understand that, but Richard might need some support from you. He's probably really scared.'

'I suppose I wouldn't mind seeing him to see what he has to say for himself, but he'll probably lie. He's good at that. I don't know if I want to stay married to him.'

Kate was quite shocked. Sophie and Richard had only been married for a year and yet she was already giving up on their marriage.

Eve had been listening to the conversation and wished she could tell Kate the truth about Sophie and Lawrence, but she knew she couldn't. It wouldn't be fair on either Sophie or Richard.

'Look — elephants to the right,' Adhama called.

Cameras came out as usual and from then on, everybody concentrated on the game drive. There was so much to see that they all put the events of the last few days to the back of their minds.

When they arrived back at the lodge, Eve saw Gary at the reception desk and decided that there was no time like the present to talk to him. David was involved in a conversation with Adhama, so this was her chance.

She walked over to the desk and Gary turned just when she reached him.

'Ms Masters, what can I do for you?' he said, sounding pleasant enough.

'There's no need to pretend with me, Gary. I know you gave the police information about me. You were trying to get me into trouble, weren't you? I can see right through you. Luckily I have an alibi so they know I couldn't have vandalised the Fergusons' room.'

'Well, that's all right, then.'

'I hope you're not threatening my wife again,' David said, striding over.

'I was doing nothing of the sort. I presume you know about the hunting.

Well, it's all legal.'

'That's all well and good, but you still spoke to the police about Eve.'

'All I did was mention the fact that she knew about Ken going out on a hunt. The police formed their own opinions.'

'I don't believe you. All I want is for you to leave my wife alone. Do you understand?'

'Perfectly, Mr Baker,' Gary said, with no remorse at all in his voice.

'Come on, Eve,' David said. 'Let's go.'

Eve followed him, surprisingly proud that her husband had stood up for her. She couldn't believe she actually liked it. It made such a change from her always being the aggressive one.

* * *

'I told you that I would speak to Gary, Eve,' David said when they got back to their room.

'I know, but I saw him and I couldn't

stop myself. After all, he did try to incriminate me.'

'I know, but Eve, I worry about you. You always rush into things without thinking.'

'But I had been thinking; ever since the police interviewed me. Anyway, it doesn't really matter. You came and rescued me and I was so proud of you. You really are wonderful, David. I do so love you.'

David couldn't be cross with her any more. He took her in his arms.

'I love you too, Eve.' His lips met hers.

The passion was still there, even though they had been together for three years. David took Eve's hand and led her to bed.

16

The following two days went by with nothing out of the ordinary happening. Everybody went on the arranged game drives and had a great time.

Sophie was looking happier than she had since the first day of the holiday. Eve thought it was possibly because she wasn't under the threat of being hit by Richard.

Still, she had claimed to still love him. If she really did have feelings for him, wouldn't she be more upset or want to go and see him?

The police had departed without even asking Sophie if she wanted to go to Dar es Salaam to see her husband. As far as she knew, he was still in hospital, but she guessed that it wouldn't be long before they transferred him to a prison.

Even Eve was more relaxed, although

she was keeping an eye on Ken and Gary. However, they didn't disappear together as they had done before. If they did, she knew it would mean that they were going on another hunt.

She was relieved that no more animals were being killed by Ken, although she knew that there were a lot of other people hunting for the fun of it. Eve couldn't understand how people could get pleasure out of killing another living being.

Eve wondered if perhaps Ken had been put off going on another hunt after his room had been vandalised. She hoped so. Perhaps he did have a bit of a conscience after all.

However, she wanted more than anything to expose Gary for the fraud he was. The only problem was that he was dangerous. If she did anything to bring him down, she was well aware that he wouldn't let her get away with it without retaliating.

★   ★   ★

Another morning arrived; it was the day on which the group were moving to the Ngorongoro Crater. They were all excited, including Sophie, who seemed to have relaxed even more.

The crater was home to a large concentration of wildlife and they all were hoping to see their first rhino of the trip.

Eve, Sophie and Kate chatted for most of the journey, while Karen kept the attention of Gary. David and James talked a little, but mostly looked out of the window watching the wildlife.

Joan and Ken sat silently, as did Joyce. She was a bit of a loner, although she did sometimes join Joan and Ken for meals.

The journey was long and most of the group eventually fell asleep. Eve tried to take a nap, but she couldn't drop off. She had started to think again about Sophie and was a little worried about her attitude. She didn't seem at all concerned about Richard. Did she care at all what happened to him? It was only a couple of days ago that Sophie had admitted to still loving Richard.

Eventually, Eve managed to banish Sophie from her thoughts and she concentrated on the game drives to come. She was looking forward to visiting the crater and wished they didn't have to wait until the following day to go on a game drive.

It was too late to go out once they arrived at their lodge, so instead they all went to their rooms to relax before dinner.

Once in their room, Eve started talking.

'Everyone seems so calm now. It seems as if nothing awful has happened on this trip, doesn't it, darling?'

'Nobody has mentioned Lawrence for a couple of days, have they?' David replied.

'They all seem to have forgotten him.'

'You're right, but perhaps it's prefer-able this way. It's best left to the police.'

Eve knew David was right, but she didn't want to leave it to the police. She wanted to be involved. It was too interesting a case to give up on.

'Has Sophie said what she's going to do at the end of the Tanzanian trip?' David asked Eve.

'She and Richard were going to Mombasa to relax, like us. Do you think she'll go back home or still go to Mombasa? I'm surprised she hasn't gone to Dar es Salaam to see Richard.'

'She told me that she doesn't want to be in Dar es Salaam on her own. A few days ago she said she still had feelings for Richard, but today in the Jeep she said she didn't care what happened to him. I think she's a bit confused. Perhaps she was really in love with Lawrence and realised that she had made a mistake marrying Richard.'

'Do you think the police can force her to stay here in Tanzania?' David asked.

Eve was surprised that David was showing this amount of interest in the case. She took advantage of it by continuing the conversation.

'I don't suppose so. Unless they suspect that she was involved in Lawrence's murder.'

'That's not very likely, if she still had feelings for him rather than Richard. Even if she didn't, why should she kill him?'

'You're suddenly taking an interest in this case, aren't you?' Eve said with a smile on her face.

'No, I'm not,' David replied abruptly. 'I was just saying . . . '

Eve smiled again. She'd get David interested in mysteries if it was the last thing she did.

'Oh David, you're so sweet,' she said, giving him a hug and kissing him.

★   ★   ★

The seating at dinner was little different from that on the bus. Gary and Karen were together as usual, which still worried Eve. However, she had decided

191

that she wasn't going to interfere in their relationship any more. There was no way she could stop Karen from liking Gary, apart perhaps from telling her about his hunting business.

Mind you, there was always the chance that Karen was so in love with Gary that she wouldn't be put off even by that. To top it all, Eve knew that the revelation would make Gary extremely angry. He could do goodness knows what to her to punish her for letting the cat out of the bag.

Anyway, if she knew Gary as well as she thought she did, he wouldn't ask Karen to stay with him in Africa. He definitely wasn't the settling down type.

Joyce joined Joan and Ken for dinner. Eve was surprised that Joan had been so quiet during the last few days. Perhaps the vandalism of their room had hit her hard. In one way she felt sorry for her, but she wasn't upset that it had happened.

Ken deserved no respect from anyone. He hunted innocent animals and Eve wanted him punished — much more so than Richard. David would say she was getting her priorities wrong, but Eve could never see it that way.

Eve and David sat with Kate, James and Sophie during dinner. Sophie seemed quite light-hearted and Eve was now seriously concerned about her. She didn't seem to realise how grave the situation was.

On top of everything, she had abandoned her husband. What must the poor man be thinking, stuck in a foreign hospital under police guard?

Of course, there was the situation between Lawrence and Sophie. If she had loved him, she was now hiding it very well. She was certainly not grieving for anyone. Eve wondered if perhaps Sophie was incapable of loving anybody.

'It will be nice to relax in Mombasa,' Sophie said, taking Eve away from her thoughts. 'I've had enough of seeing wildlife.'

Eve was startled to hear that Sophie

intended to go to Mombasa rather than seeing Richard or going home, but she hid her feelings.

'But tomorrow should be fantastic in the crater,' she exclaimed. 'David and I can't wait. We're so hoping to see a rhino.'

David nodded in agreement.

'I must say, I'm looking forward to it very much as well,' Kate said.

'I only did this safari to please Richard, and now he's gone.' Sophie looked around defiantly.

Eve had had enough.

'He's not *gone*,' she said in exasperation. 'He's in hospital under armed guard and has been abandoned by you.'

As she felt her anger rising, Eve forgot about hiding what she thought. It wasn't an open and shut case, and if David was in the same situation as Richard, she wouldn't leave him for a minute. She had been sympathetic towards Sophie, but now the woman was openly revelling in her newfound freedom!

Sophie now looked as if she were about to cry.

'I thought you were my friend, Eve. I don't want any dinner now. I'm going to my room.'

With that, she got up and almost ran out of the dining room.

'I didn't mean to upset her, but she has gone from being terrified about the situation to just not caring. She almost seems happy. Perhaps I should go after her?'

'No,' Kate said. 'I'll go and see her. Let her calm down first. I'll take her some food later.'

'OK,' Eve agreed, relieved. 'It's better that she cools down a bit. Perhaps I'll apologise to her tomorrow, though I don't really think I have anything to say sorry about.'

David was amazed that Eve might actually say she was sorry — not that she really needed to. Sophie was acting very erratically, and he thought she might still be in shock — or perhaps she really didn't care about anyone except herself.

When Kate came back from seeing Sophie, Eve asked how she was.

'She seems to have got over what you said. She gave me the impression that there was nothing wrong.'

'But she's not coming back to join us?'

'No, she said she wanted to be on her own.'

Eve felt a bit guilty, but she did think there was something odd about Sophie. Was she really as innocent in this as she claimed to be?

She decided however, that it was best to leave it be for the time being and enjoy the meal.

17

The following morning, Eve was up early yet again — but this time it was not because she couldn't sleep. She was excited about the game drive in the crater.

For a change, she had slept well and was ready for action. She had even put Sophie and her contrariness to the back of her mind.

Everyone in the group was waiting for the Jeep — that is, everyone except for Sophie. Eve was worried. Had she upset her to the extent that Sophie didn't want to see her?

'Do you think we should go and find her?' Eve asked Kate. 'She wasn't at breakfast.'

'She wasn't that keen on coming, so she's probably resting.'

'I still think I should go and see if she's coming. I think I owe her an apology anyway. Gary's not here yet so I have a few minutes.'

Kate nodded.

'Do you want me to come with you?'

'No, it's all right. I'll only be a minute.'

Eve dashed to Sophie's room, not wanting to delay everybody else. She was quite proud of herself. She was actually being considerate to other people. David definitely was a good influence on her.

Eve knocked at the door three times, but there was no reply. She tried the door, and to her surprise it opened.

'Sophie,' Eve called as she entered.

There was still no reply. Eve moved towards the bed and saw Sophie lying there, eyes closed.

'Sophie, we're off to the crater. Are you coming?'

She didn't reply so Eve bent down and shook her. She could, after all, be in a deep sleep. However, when Sophie didn't move, Eve started to get worried. She shook her again, but nothing.

Eve felt for her pulse and was relieved to find one. However, there was definitely something wrong with her.

Eve rushed back to the group. Gary was there looking impatient.

'At last, Ms Masters, we are about to leave.'

'You can't leave,' Eve exclaimed. 'There's something wrong. Sophie won't wake up.'

Gary looked shocked.

'She's not dead?'

'No, I felt her pulse.'

Gary started to head over to Sophie's room, followed by the whole group.

'You don't all need to come,' he said, glancing back in annoyance.

'Yes, we do,' Eve said, speaking for everyone.

Gary entered Sophie's room, followed by Eve and Kate. Everyone else crowded into the doorway.

Gary shook Sophie, but nothing. Eve wandered into the bathroom.

'Gary,' she shouted. 'There's an empty pill box and packet in here. I don't believe it. I think she's taken an overdose.'

'Let me have a look at the box,' Gary said.

Eve came out of the bathroom, looking pale. She was almost in tears. Was this her fault? She handed the box to Gary and he studied it.

'These are pretty strong sleeping tablets. They can knock you out. Perhaps she took one too many. Let's not assume that she tried to take her own life.'

Eve didn't feel reassured. Looking at David who was at the door, she spoke.

'It's my fault. I was horrible to her last night so she went and took an overdose.'

'Don't be silly, darling,' David said to her, entering the room and taking his wife into his arms. 'She was behaving strangely. I said she was likely to still be in shock. And as Gary said, it was probably an accident.'

'This is all well and good,' Gary said. 'But there's no time to waste. I'm going to call the air ambulance so we can get her to a hospital in Dar es Salaam. I think you should all go on the game drive without me.'

'We can't just leave Sophie,' Eve said.

'Yes, we can,' David replied. 'There's nothing we can do. She'll be in good hands.'

Eve nodded, even though she wanted to go to Dar es Salaam with Sophie. She still felt it was her fault . . . but then she had another thought.

Gary could be right in that she hadn't taken an overdose — but maybe Sophie hadn't made a mistake either. Perhaps somebody had tried to murder her, but wanted it to look like suicide.

However Eve had no idea why anyone would want to kill her, particularly amongst the group.

Luckily, Dar es Salaam was next on the tour agenda, so she would get to see Sophie soon, all being well. Unfortunately, she probably wouldn't be allowed to see Richard.

Everyone started to move out of

Sophie's room. They were all sombre and they said little as they boarded the Jeep. Even Joan was quiet.

* * *

The game drive turned out to be better than expected. Nobody was really in the mood for doing anything, but as the Jeep bumped and jolted its way down into the crater, the excitement began to build.

'Look, giraffes over there,' Adhama said as everyone got their cameras out.

In the end, the group got to see all of the Big Five; a pride of lions, four elephants, one leopard, a herd of buffalo, and what Eve wanted to see the most, the elusive rhinoceros.

There were, in fact, three adults and one baby rhino. Eve was delighted as was everyone else, but she couldn't help remembering that these amazing creatures were hunted just for their horns. It would be a real tragedy if the species were wiped out simply due to greed.

Eve glanced at Ken, who was happily taking photos and pointing at the animals. She felt sick. What a hypocrite he was. For that one moment she forgot about Sophie.

'We've got some wonderful photos on this holiday, haven't we, darling?' Kate said to James.

'We have, and despite the unrest, it has been a fabulous trip.'

'Yes, we've got lots of great photos as well,' Eve agreed with Kate and James, but then she thought about Sophie again. She remembered seeing her lying in bed and the shiver of fear that ran through her when she thought that Sophie might be dead.

'It's a pity Sophie missed this drive,' she said.

'She wasn't madly keen on the wildlife. It was Richard's dream holiday, not hers,' David replied.

'Yes, poor Richard,' Kate said. 'I can't imagine him as a murderer, but then looks can be deceptive. Though why he would have wanted to kill

Lawrence, I don't know.'

Eve shrugged, even though she knew full well that Richard had a motive to kill him.

'I wish I could have gone to Dar es Salaam with Sophie,' she whispered to David. 'I feel so guilty.'

'You have nothing to feel guilty about, darling,' David replied. 'I hardly think that Sophie took an overdose because of what you said. If she really did try and kill herself, which I somehow doubt, it's not your fault. Anyhow, you promised not to get involved in any more mysteries and you've been good to your word. I'm proud of you.'

Eve smiled, but inside, her mind was in turmoil. She was involved already and she wanted to get more involved. She wanted to find out if Richard really was a murderer.

She had an awful feeling that the police wouldn't look any further, and he would go to jail whether he had killed Lawrence or not.

*   *   *

After three hours the Jeep returned to the lodge. Karen bounded out straight away, right in to Gary's arms. Eve took no notice of her display of affection, but marched straight up to Gary.

'Any news about Sophie?' she asked.

'She's been taken to the hospital, but I don't know any more at this moment,' he said, pushing Karen away.

Eve noticed this and wondered if he was trying to finish their relationship now that it was nearly the end of the safari. Gary wouldn't be joining them in Mombasa as this part of the trip was simply a beach holiday and no guide was needed.

Karen looked a little hurt and Eve actually felt like giving her a hug, rather than saying 'I told you so.' However, she restrained herself. After all, Gary might simply have pushed her away because Eve had come to talk to him.

'You will let me know if there is any

news about Sophie, won't you, Gary?'

'Yes, of course.'

Eve was quite surprised that he was so cooperative after her previous encounter with him. However, despite his politeness, she hadn't forgotten that he ran hunting safaris. She was going to expose him and destroy that evil business of his if it was the last thing she did.

★   ★   ★

When Eve and David came down for dinner, she noticed Ken talking to Gary. They couldn't be arranging another hunt, could they? There was only one more day at the crater before heading off to Dar es Salaam.

Eve's blood boiled. She'd had enough of keeping quiet and letting Gary get away with what he was doing.

That evening, everybody sat together around a big table. The talk was mainly about what they had seen that day in the crater. Eve was finding it hard to join in. She was getting angrier and angrier with Gary.

All of a sudden, she spoke out loudly.

'Did you know that Gary runs a hunting business as well as this holiday company?'

Everyone went quiet, even Gary, who was sitting next to Karen. It was she who spoke first.

'I don't believe you, Eve. Gary loves animals.'

'Really? I know for a fact that he has taken Ken out for a hunt.'

'What's it got to do with you?' Joan spoke angrily.

'We've all come here to admire the animals, not to kill them.' Eve spoke sharply.

'If I'd known this, I would have chosen a different holiday company,' Kate said.

'The hunts are all legal.' Gary finally spoke, keeping his cool.

'What difference does that make?' Kate continued. 'You're still killing animals, some of which are probably endangered. Why didn't you tell us this before, Eve?'

'Gary threatened me, but when I saw him talking to Ken earlier today, I was so angry. They were probably arranging another hunt.'

'Well, this is very disappointing,' James said. 'I thought we were coming on holiday with an animal lover, not one who condones hunting. I certainly will not be recommending this company to my friends.'

'I doubt if it will affect my bookings that much.'

'It will do if we flood social media with posts against you,' Eve spoke.

'My holiday business is not as remunerative as the hunting side, so I'm sure I'll survive.'

Karen was crying throughout all of this.

Gary spoke to her.

'I'm sorry to disappoint you, Karen — but that's life, honey.'

'I hate you,' she shouted, pushed her

chair back and stumbled away from the dining table.

'Now look what you've done, Eve. Shattered all her illusions,' Gary spoke angrily.

'They were going to be shattered anyway. I can't see you inviting her to stay with you in Africa.'

'You're right, but I would have been gentler about it. I would have let her go back with lots of happy memories.'

'She wouldn't have been happy unless you asked her to stay here with you.'

'I think it's better if I dined at another table.'

'Too right,' Eve responded.

As Gary got up, Joan and Ken did as well, leaving just Eve, David, Kate, James and Joyce. Eve hadn't had much to do with Joyce, but it was she who spoke first.

'I'm shocked. I wouldn't have come with this holiday company either, had I known. And to actually go hunting during a safari! It's hard to believe that

Joan and Ken are involved in hunting. I know you didn't get on with Joan, Eve, but they were both very pleasant to me.'

David spoke at last. He had kept silent throughout the whole exchange.

'That was very brave of you, Eve.'

'Or foolhardy,' she responded wryly.

'Gary can't really do anything now that everybody knows, though what he was going to do to you, I don't know.'

'Kill me, probably. If you can kill animals, it shouldn't be so hard to kill a person.'

Eve shivered. Perhaps he might still do something to her, even though he would look like the obvious culprit. He was probably very good at covering his tracks.

'Come on, let's get some food from the buffet,' James said. 'At least we haven't got Gary with us for much longer.'

Everyone nodded and murmured in agreement.

As Eve went to the buffet table, she saw Gary talking to Hamisi. He was obviously part of the hunting business. Suddenly, Eve felt relieved. She was glad that she had exposed Gary's dark secret to the others, even though there were only a few of them. She planned to do more when she got home.

As Eve walked back to her table, she caught Gary's eye. His face was devoid of all expression, but his eyes bored into hers. She thought that all she could see was pure evil, and she shivered.

18

The following morning there was another game drive which proved to be fruitful. Everybody was pleased to see the group of rhinos again, together with plenty of other wildlife.

The crater really was a paradise for animals, Eve thought. If only there weren't people like Gary around.

The group was quieter than normal. Things had changed since Eve's expose of the previous day. Nobody spoke to Joan and Ken, and Eve was surprised they had turned up for the game drive. She thought how brazen they were. They didn't seem to care what other people thought of them.

More importantly, there was no Gary. Adhama said he wasn't well, but Eve thought differently. He had alienated the people on the safari, but Eve doubted he was embarrassed. He couldn't see that he was doing anything wrong and was probably avoiding everybody because he couldn't be bothered to argue with them.

Karen came and sat near to Eve and David.

'You were right about Gary, Eve. I should have listened to you.'

'Don't beat yourself up about it, Karen. I've done my fair share of rushing into things without thinking of the consequences. However, I am really sorry that this has happened to you.'

'Thanks. I'm sure I'll get over it, but for the moment it hurts. Gary is a completely different man to the one I thought he was.'

'Aren't you a little scared of what Gary might do to you, Eve?' Joyce asked. 'After all, you said that he did threaten you.'

'If anything happened to me, I think he would look like the most obvious culprit. I'm not too worried.'

David looked at Eve and he knew that secretly she was a tiny bit afraid.

She had more or less admitted it the previous evening.

David had said very little to Eve about the incident. In one way, he was proud of her. Hunting shouldn't be condoned and he loved the fact that she had stood up for the welfare of animals and for what she believed in.

However, he was a little concerned for her safety. If Gary ran a hunting business, he probably hunted himself. Would he stop at killing animals? Would he not find it relatively easy to kill someone who stood in the way of his making money?

* * *

After lunch, everybody was waiting outside the lodge with their bags, ready to leave for Dar es Salaam. Then Gary appeared, but nobody spoke to him and he avoided eye contact with all of them. Karen moved to stand near Eve.

Eve whispered to Karen, 'Has Gary

tried to explain his actions or has he avoided you?'

'He did try to talk to me in the lobby last night, but I rushed back to the restaurant. You were all there, so I felt safe. However, I feel so foolish. I just threw myself at him, not knowing anything about him.'

Eve spoke sympathetically. 'You're not foolish at all. You were swept away by a very handsome and exciting man. Goodness knows I've done it myself enough times.'

'Yes, but I bet none of them were as bad as Gary,' Karen said, tears welling up in her eyes.

Eve couldn't disagree with her, so instead put her arm around her and gave her a little squeeze. She was glad when the Jeep turned up as she couldn't think of anything else to say to console Karen; only time could heal the wounds.

Everybody boarded the Jeep. When they had all sat down, Eve spoke to David.

'I can't wait to get to Dar es Salaam. We have to go and see Sophie in the hospital.'

His face darkened. 'Is it a good idea to get even more involved, Eve?'

David didn't want Eve to see Sophie or anyone else who could be involved in the murder of Lawrence. Next thing, she would be wanting to see Richard.

'I can't *not* go and see her. She might be a little strange, but we have become friends over the last few days. She's probably feeling scared and alone. She needs to know she's not been deserted. She was terrified of being on her own in Dar es Salaam.'

David sighed. 'Fair enough, Eve, but you know how I worry about you.'

'I promise I won't do anything stupid.'

David squeezed Eve's hand to reassure her that he was behind her. Inside, he was in turmoil. What would Eve get herself into next?

★ ★ ★

It was evening when the group reached Dar es Salaam. They were just in time for dinner, so they all stowed their cases in their rooms and went straight to the restaurant. Gary was conspicuous by his absence. He wasn't really needed any more, but Eve knew that wasn't the reason why he wasn't around. He hadn't spoken to anyone on the journey, not even Joan and Ken.

Karen looked depressed at dinner and Eve tried to cheer her up.

'You know, if you really want to come and live in Africa, there's lots of voluntary work you could do,' she suggested.

'I suppose so, but I don't think I want to come here any more.'

Eve nodded. Karen had been looking for romance in an exciting country, not to get her hands dirty. She couldn't really blame her.

Eve wouldn't want to do voluntary work herself. She donated plenty of money to charities, but that was as far as she felt she could go.

However, she could try to do something to stop the hunting of animals. She grew quiet over dinner, mulling over ideas, and excused herself early, saying she wanted to check emails. She told David to stay and was pleased when he agreed. She wanted a little time on her own.

When Eve got back to her room, she opened up her laptop and within minutes, had started a petition online with a reputable petition site. She wanted people to pledge not to book holidays with Gary's company because he also ran a hunting business. She knew that it could be dangerous, but she didn't care. Something had to be done.

A few minutes after posting the petition, people had already begun to sign.

Eve smiled to herself. Another step had been taken in the fight against hunting. The only thing she decided not to do was tell David. After all, why worry him?

19

Next day there were excursions on offer, but Eve wanted only to go and see Sophie in hospital. Surprisingly David didn't argue with her, although Eve was certain he didn't want to go with her — or even for her to go at all.

She almost told him he needn't come, but she knew he would worry and would probably refuse to stay behind.

In a way, she thought it would be better to go alone. It would give her the opportunity to try and get in to see Richard. She knew David would stop her doing that, even before the police guard did.

Not knowing whether Gary had seen the petition on the internet, Eve sent David to ask him which hospital Sophie was in. She thought it highly unlikely that he would have found out about the petition yet, but she didn't want a confrontation with him this morning. It did cross her mind that he might say something to David, but it was a risk she was prepared to take.

When David came back, he didn't mention the petition and just told her the name of the hospital. Eve was relieved. No doubt both Gary and David would find out about the petition sooner or later, but she hoped it would be later rather than sooner.

It didn't cross her mind that it might cause fewer arguments if she told David now instead of keeping the secret from him.

★   ★   ★

It didn't take long for a taxi to arrive to take Eve and David to the hospital. Eve thought how different it was to be in a city again after spending so much time out in the bush. She was already quite enjoying the experience. Much as she loved wildlife, she was a city girl at heart.

However, the traffic was crawling and Eve became frustrated. She was keen to get to the hospital to see Sophie and didn't want to waste time in a traffic jam. Her mind was working overtime. Did Sophie really try to kill herself? Had she been able to see Richard? What was the state of her mind now?

Finally, the taxi arrived at the hospital and they were on their way to Sophie's room. It was lucky that the woman at the reception desk spoke English.

Entering Sophie's room, they saw her sitting up in bed looking vacantly at the wall. When she turned, Eve was pleased to see her smile.

'Eve, David, it's so good to see you. It's horrible here.'

'What's wrong with it? It all seems clean and tidy,' Eve said. 'They were very helpful at reception, too.'

'It's not that. It's being alone in a strange country.'

'I can understand that,' Eve paused, a

little nervous to ask the next question with David there. Still, she had to do it.

'Have they let you see Richard?'

'Once. He swears he didn't do it — you know, kill Lawrence.'

'Do you believe him?'

'I really don't know. He seems genuine enough, but who else had reason to kill him?'

Eve agreed with Sophie, even though she knew Gary had reason to kill Lawrence. She decided to change the subject.

'I hate to bring this up, but why did you take an overdose?'

'I didn't mean to. I was feeling a bit down and I just wanted to sleep. However, my sleeping tablets weren't working, so I took extra. It was stupid, I know. They are pretty strong, but I thought if the first ones hadn't worked, I should be OK taking more. Unfortunately they knocked me out.'

'That's a relief. I felt a bit guilty saying what I did last night. I thought I was to blame for you taking the tablets.'

'Don't be silly. It would take more than that.'

Eve squeezed Sophie's hand.

'When are they letting you out of here?'

'Later today when I've seen the psychiatrist again. She's convinced that I did try and take an overdose and will have to agree that I'm well enough to leave.'

'What are you going to do then?'

'Rejoin the tour.'

Eve was quite shocked that Sophie still planned to have a holiday.

'What about Richard?'

'Our marriage is over whatever. I've realised I loved Lawrence more than Richard, and although he's gone, I know I can't stay with my husband, even if he's proved innocent.'

Just as Sophie finished speaking, the psychiatrist came in.

'We'll wait outside, Sophie,' Eve said. 'You can come to the hotel with us.'

Sophie nodded and Eve and David left.

'You were very quiet, David,' Eve said.

'I let you talk to her as I thought she'd find it easier than talking to me.'

'What did you make of her?'

'I thought that Sophie was very calm, too calm in fact. She was very irrational before.'

'You're right. That's exactly what I thought. I think she's hiding something . . .'

Eve almost said that she was going to find out, but she stopped herself. David would think that she was interfering. Instead they both went to sit down, quiet and lost in their own thoughts.

David was wondering how he could stop Eve from getting even more involved, while Eve was trying to figure out what Sophie was hiding. She was convinced Sophie had secrets, but what they were she didn't know.

* * *

Sophie joined Eve and David for dinner, as did Kate and James. No one else from the group was there when they entered the restaurant. Eve had been hoping to catch Karen and invite her to eat with them now that her relationship with Gary was at an end.

Almost as soon as they had given their orders to the waiter, Gary came storming in to the restaurant.

'You, Ms Masters, have really gone too far this time. Take that petition off the internet now.'

'I haven't got my computer handy, and even if I did have, I wouldn't. Hunting is barbaric and cruel and should be stopped.'

'What petition is this?' David asked, perplexed.

He was confused. He hadn't heard anything about a petition. What was Eve up to now?

'Your wife has put a petition online asking people to pledge to never use my holiday company because I also run a hunting business.'

'Eve, why didn't you tell me about this?'

Eve was relieved to hear that he didn't sound angry — or perhaps he wasn't really showing his feelings.

'I'm sorry, David. I didn't want you to worry.'

'You're the one who should worry, Ms Masters,' Gary growled.

'How dare you threaten my wife!' David exclaimed, jumping up.

Eve couldn't have been prouder of David at that moment. For once in her life, she didn't mind being protected.

However, Gary ignored David and continued talking to Eve.

'I refuse to be destroyed by some English busybody, so beware, Ms Masters.'

With that he stormed off, bumping into Karen as he left. She refused to look him in the eye.

'Are you all right, Eve?' Kate asked.

'Yes, I'm fine, just angry. How dare he threaten me again? David, you were wonderful; thank you.'

'I just wish you'd told me, Eve. I think a petition is a good idea, although I would have preferred it if you had waited and started the petition in England. You'll be far away from Gary then.'

'I'm sure he could get to me anywhere in the world, so it makes no difference.'

'I think it's commendable what you've done, but aren't you a little scared of what Gary might do to you, Eve?' James asked.

'No, not really. I don't for one minute think that my petition will put him out of business, but it might cause some damage. What's he going to do, anyway? Kill me?'

'Don't say that, Eve! We've been in this position before,' David exclaimed. 'I couldn't bear to lose you — not just after we've got married.'

'You won't get away with losing me that easily, darling.'

David smiled, but inside he was apprehensive. Gary seemed to have no scruples and was unpredictable. He put on a good show of being a lover of animals, but the opposite was the truth.

227

David wouldn't put it past him to get his revenge in some way.

However, too many people had heard his threats so it would be a giveaway if something happened to Eve. At least, he hoped so.

Karen came up to the table.

'Can I join you?' she asked shyly.

'Of course,' Eve replied. 'I was looking for you earlier.'

'I was having a nap. What's been going on with Gary?'

Eve told her.

'Where do I sign?' Karen asked. 'He deserves all that he gets.' There was venom in her voice.

'I think you're making too much of this. The man has to make a living,' Sophie said.

Eve was shocked.

'I didn't think you approved of hunting, Sophie?'

'Well, I suppose I don't, but I do believe in live and let live. It's really none of our business.'

'Live and let live?' Eve exclaimed,

banging her hand on the table. 'That's the last thing Gary is doing. We can't just close our eyes to all the evil that's going on in this world. People have to stand up for what they believe in and what is right.'

David could see how agitated Eve was becoming.

'Eve, calm down,' he said. 'Everybody is entitled to their own opinion.'

'Even if it's the wrong one?'

The group was then interrupted by the starters arriving. Karen, who had arrived late, decided just to order a main course. The rest all started eating in silence, even Sophie, who didn't seem fazed by Eve's outburst.

'I'm looking forward to the rest in Mombasa,' Kate piped up when they had finished their starters, hoping to break the silence. 'It will make a change from getting up at the crack of dawn to go wildlife spotting.'

'I'm just looking forward to getting out of Tanzania after all that's happened,' Sophie said.

'Don't you think you should stay to give Richard some support?' Kate asked, amazed that Sophie was planning to leave.

Sophie tossed her head. 'Our marriage is over. I don't want to see him again.'

Eve, for once, kept quiet, which was probably a good thing after her outburst. However, she felt that even if Sophie didn't love Richard any more, she could at least give him some support in this strange, foreign land. She wouldn't ever desert David, even if they weren't a couple any more — not that she ever expected to be without him.

Eve's decision not to reply to Sophie's comments was a relief to David. Things were tense enough already.

Kate was very diplomatic and started talking about their safari. As the main courses arrived, everyone seemed more relaxed — everyone, that is, apart from Eve. She was still angry at Sophie's attitude, but she knew that it was best left alone.

The rest of the dinner went by pleasantly enough, although Eve was quieter than normal, leaving the others to chat.

All she knew was that there was something not right with Sophie — and she had to find out what it was.

20

Eve and David were up early the following day as they had booked a tour of Dar es Salaam. When they entered the restaurant, they saw that the only other people from their group who were having breakfast were Joan and Ken.

They nodded and Eve was amazed that they had acknowledged them — especially as she thought that Gary might have told them about her petition.

Eve and David sat down to order their coffees and then went to the breakfast buffet. As usual there was a great choice for Eve. She wished that vegetarian food was as creative on Crete as it was here.

As they sat down, Sophie breezed in and came and sat with them without asking. Eve was very surprised after what had happened the previous evening.

'I've decided to take this tour that you're doing, Eve, otherwise I'll be sitting here twisting my thumbs all day. You don't mind, do you?'

'No, why should I?' Eve replied, trying to sound light-hearted.

'Well, we did fall out a bit last night, didn't we, but it's all water under the bridge now.'

'Yes, of course,' Eve replied.

She decided to keep the peace, more than a little interested to see how Sophie acted today. She seemed to have changed from being frightened and nervous in to a much stronger woman.

'You're definitely not going to see Richard again, then?' David asked, thinking it better if he asked the question rather than Eve. He believed she could easily rub Sophie up the wrong way.

'No — as I said, it's over between us. The police don't seem to want anything from me, so I shall go to Mombasa as planned and relax before flying home.'

Eve didn't say anything, and David

wondered what was going on in that complicated brain of hers.

James and Kate came in to the restaurant and Eve waved. They came over and sat down.

'Are you going on the tour today?' Sophie asked.

'No, we went yesterday. We're just going to relax today. We've had so many early starts, we woke at six out of habit.'

When Sophie went up to the buffet to get her breakfast, Kate turned to Eve.

'Sophie's talking to you, then?'

'Yes, she's all sweetness and light today as if nothing happened. I really can't make her out.'

'Me neither. I still can't get over the fact that she won't stay here to give Richard moral support — unless, of course, she really thinks that he is the murderer.'

'That could be it, I suppose,' replied Eve, although she felt that Sophie simply didn't care.

'I can't imagine what it would be like

to think that your partner was capable of killing someone.'

'Me neither.'

Sophie came back, her plate piled high.

'I'm starving. The hospital food is as awful here as it is in England. Not that I've been to a National Health hospital for years. Private is so much better.'

'It's a good thing you were only there for a short time then.' Eve smiled, ignoring her statement about the National Health Service. Yes, Eve went private, but she appreciated the fact that there was free health care for everyone. Not every country could boast that.

'I couldn't have endured the hospital for much longer. It's so nice to be out. I'm going to make the most of the next week.'

Eve wondered what she meant by that. What could Sophie get up to in Mombasa?

* * *

Eve was shocked to see Gary board the tour bus. He completely ignored her and David and sat two seats in front of them, next to Sophie.

Eve was surprised that he didn't say anything to her. He couldn't have forgotten about the petition — or had he decided that it wouldn't do him that much harm?

There were a few other people on the bus from different hotels. They were quite noisy, so David and Eve relaxed and didn't bother to chat.

Anyway, Eve had too much to think about. Was Richard really the killer? Did Gary have any plans to get rid of her? Why was Sophie so laid back now? Her mind was in turmoil.

She looked towards the front of the bus. Sophie and Gary seemed to be deep in conversation, and every now and then she heard them laugh. Something about the situation was off, and Eve's busy brain was working nineteen to the dozen.

Was Gary making a pass at Sophie? If

so, she didn't seem to mind. Eve wished she had been able to see Richard in hospital. She would then have been able to observe the situation from his point of view.

He didn't seem like a killer to her, but then the most unlikely people turned out to be murderers, she knew through personal experience.

When the bus stopped at the National Museum, Sophie went off with Gary without saying anything to Eve and David. Eve was dumbfounded. They had had very little to do with each other throughout the holiday, but now they seemed as if they were close friends.

'Let's follow them, David,' Eve said. 'There's something fishy going on there.'

'Eve, don't be silly. They're bound to see us, and anyway, why?'

'Don't you think it's a bit strange that she's gone wandering off with Gary?'

'A little, perhaps, but maybe they

have things to talk about, what with her husband being arrested.'

'But she more or less said that she doesn't care. What is there to talk about?'

'I don't know, Eve. Don't make a mountain out of a molehill.'

'I'm not. They've hardly spoken to each other the whole trip, so why now?'

'I don't know. Oh, come on, Eve, let's just enjoy the museum.'

Eve nodded reluctantly, but it wasn't long before she was engrossed in the history of Tanzania. She loved to learn as much as possible about the places she visited.

Eventually, she and David wandered off in different directions and that was when it happened. As Eve turned a corner, she caught sight of Sophie and Gary and froze. They were locked in what seemed to be a never-ending kiss.

Eve couldn't believe her eyes. How come this was happening? Sophie had told her she still loved Lawrence, despite the fact that he was dead. Now she was kissing Gary. When on earth had this started? It must have happened virtually overnight.

Eve had to admit to herself that she was shocked — and not much shocked Eve Masters.

As Gary and Sophie parted, he glanced over her shoulder to where Eve was standing.

Not really knowing if Gary had seen her or not, Eve turned and went the other way. Had he noticed her watching them, or was her imagination playing tricks on her?

David suddenly appeared and put his arm around Eve. She jumped.

'What's up, darling? You look as if you've just seen a ghost.'

'Do I? You just gave me a fright, that's all,' she said putting her arms around David.

'I do love you, you know.'

'Me too,' he replied, kissing her very gently so as not to ruin her lipstick. Eve was always so meticulous with her make-up and dress.

She decided not to tell David that she had seen Gary and Sophie kissing. He would probably tell her to stop interfering, although she imagined he would be as surprised as her.

They wandered off looking at the artefacts, but Eve had lost interest. All she could think about was Sophie with Gary.

When they got back on the bus, Gary didn't acknowledge them again. Eve was a little worried. She was feeling pretty certain now that Gary had seen her watching him kiss Sophie. What would he do about it?

A shiver of fear ran down her spine. She was becoming more and more embroiled in Gary's life and she was sure it wasn't a good thing.

21

In the hospital, Richard was still lying with his broken leg raised in the air. He was in considerable pain, despite having been given painkillers.

However, he was relieved to be in hospital and not in a police cell. He was sure that would be awful. Unfortunately he knew he wouldn't be able to stay in the hospital for ever.

His thoughts were in a muddle. He didn't know what he had been thinking when he had tried to escape from the police. How on earth could he have imagined that he could actually get out of the Serengeti on his own?

Where would he have gone, anyway? He would be lost in this country. On top of everything, his botched escape made him look guilty, and he wasn't. It hadn't crossed his mind that Sophie was still interested in Lawrence, so why should he kill him?

Not that he would have killed him even if she had carried a torch for the man. That would have been an extreme reaction. He wasn't a murderer.

Now he wasn't sure if Sophie and Lawrence had been planning to run away together. The previous day Sophie had told him she wanted a divorce. There had been no sign of this before. It destroyed him that she didn't love him any more. Richard didn't know how he could prove his innocence. The police thought Lawrence and Sophie were having an affair, so the obvious culprit was himself.

He had no real alibi for the time of Lawrence's murder. He had been in bed with Sophie, but she had told the police she had been sleeping soundly thanks to her pills, so hadn't heard whether he had got up or not. She really hadn't been helpful to him at all, and that was suspicious.

'Time for a painkiller, Mr Blair,' a

male nurse said, coming into the ward with a syringe.

'An injection?' Richard asked. 'I usually have tablets.'

'This is better — more powerful.'

'Great,' Richard said. 'I could do with something stronger.'

The nurse waited until Richard fell asleep.

★　★　★

The tour was almost over and the bus was approaching the hotel. Eve was now feeling on edge. She hadn't intended telling David that she had seen Gary and Sophie kissing, but now she wondered if she was doing the right thing keeping it to herself.

She had promised David she wouldn't get involved in any more mysteries, and she thought she had done very well so far, with just one or two lapses.

Yes, she had started the petition, but in her mind that wasn't really interfering. She had started petitions about animal welfare before.

Eve's mind was still filled with so many thoughts, but she was also irritated with herself. She just couldn't work this one out.

Had Sophie and Gary just started a relationship or had this been going on for some time? What about Karen? Had Gary used her to stop people thinking that there was something going on between him and Sophie?

Perhaps Richard had killed the wrong man. Maybe it was Gary who was a threat to their marriage, not Lawrence.

She wanted to solve this puzzle, but there wasn't much time. The next day they would be travelling to Mombasa without Gary. She wondered whether Sophie would stay behind with him, or would she go with them as planned?

★　★　★

Returning to the hotel, Eve decided she was going to do a little sunbathing. David told her he would go and have a lie down in their room. He was feeling a little tired and he wasn't as keen on sunbathing as she was.

Eve went and got changed and it wasn't long before she was lying by the pool. She was just dozing off when she heard a voice whispering into her ear. She sat up quickly. It was Gary.

'What do you want?' she snapped.

He was the last person she expected to see sitting next to her and she wasn't prepared to be polite.

'I know you saw Sophie and me in the museum. You will not speak of this to anyone — or else.'

'Or else what?' Eve responded, sounding very sure of herself, even though she was nothing of the sort.

'You think you are very clever, Ms Masters, but you're not. You are in a strange country and things work differently here.'

'I live in a strange country just as you do, so I know that things work differently, but murder is murder everywhere.'

'Nobody has murdered anybody here — that is, apart from Richard.'

'I'm beginning to doubt that he really did murder Lawrence. There are far more likely suspects.'

'You had better watch what you are saying or things might end up not so good for you.'

'Are you threatening me again, Gary?'

'No, I'm just warning you.'

With that, Gary got up and walked away. Eve realised she was trembling. She had acted as if she was confident, but at the moment, she was nothing of the sort.

She leaned back on her lounger and took a couple of deep breaths. Should she tell David about this? No, it would probably be best not to. He would only worry — or perhaps he would confront Gary. Gary was dangerous and she didn't want anything to happen to David, especially if it was her fault.

She didn't want to do this, but she decided she would leave all this alone

— even if it meant that the wrong person had been arrested and could possibly go to jail for something he didn't do.

22

In the hospital, a nurse went to check up on Richard Blair.

'OK, Mr Blair, time for your medicine.'

Richard didn't move.

'Mr Blair, are you asleep?'

A trickle of blood ran down Richard's nose.

'Oh, my God,' the nurse cried out and rang the emergency bell.

* * *

Meanwhile, Eve had calmed down and managed to drift off in the sun. However, she was woken by her usual bad dream of being chased by Gary in the African bush. She was getting fed up of these nightmares. Would Gary never leave her alone, even when she was asleep?

She shook her head, telling herself that she was being stupid worrying so much. She just wouldn't do anything else; then she should be all right. Suddenly, she wanted to be in the safe and protective arms of David, so she gathered her things together and slipped on her sundress.

Eve walked into the hotel, for a moment wishing they had gone somewhere else for their honeymoon.

As she went into the lift, she felt a blow on the back of her head and she was out like a light.

★　★　★

The medical team managed to resuscitate Richard Blair. One of the nurses gasped.

'Doctor,' she said. 'He's had a nosebleed and there is bruising all over his body.'

Richard opened his mouth to say something, but all that came out was blood.

'How on earth did this happen? These are classic signs of an overdose of warfarin,' the doctor exclaimed. 'Who could have given this to him? Take some blood, nurse, and we can test it immediately. If I'm right, we will have to administer the antidote quickly before he gets worse.

'When you've done that, ring the police. This is a case of attempted murder. How the person got by the security guard, I can't imagine.'

★   ★   ★

Eve woke up in a strange place. She had no idea where she was and all she felt was a terrible pain in her head. Then she remembered that someone had hit her in the lift just as she was returning to her room. Had she been kidnapped yet again? What on earth would David think when he found her missing?

It seemed highly likely that the person who did this was Gary. He wanted her out of the way for more than one reason. It couldn't just be because of the petition. That was too small a thing to warrant a kidnapping.

Was it because she saw him kiss Sophie? Why would that worry him unless he was really the person who had killed Lawrence? Perhaps they had planned it between themselves because Lawrence wouldn't leave Sophie alone.

However, Eve hadn't seen either of them kill Lawrence, so how could she be a threat?

Eve sat up slowly, wishing that her headache would go away. She looked around the room and noticed someone sitting in the corner. The light wasn't good so she had trouble recognising him.

'Gary?' she asked.

The man stood up.

'No, it's Hamisi.'

For a moment, the name meant nothing to her, but as he walked towards her, she suddenly recognised who it was. Hamisi was the man who kept appearing wherever they went; he was the person whom she had over-heard Gary talking to back in Taita Hills. Worse, he was holding a gun.

'What do you want with me?' Eve asked, starting to tremble.

'That is up to the boss.'

'Gary, you mean?'

Hamisi just shrugged.

'I have to go now. There's a bottle of water for you on the table.'

'You're leaving me here alone?'

'You'll be fine here. All the doors will be locked so nobody will get in.'

'And I can't get out.'

'Precisely.'

Hamisi then left without another word. Eve felt like crying. How could she get out of this one?

She got up and tried the door. Then she tried the shutters on the windows, but they too were locked.

Eve sat down and took a sip of water. It was warm, but at least it quenched her thirst a little.

She hoped David would soon realise that she was missing and call the police.

However, how would they be able to find her? She had no idea where she was or how far away it was from the hotel. She had been out cold throughout the whole journey.

She was really worried now, more so then she had ever been before. For the first time, she believed she really could end up dead.

★   ★   ★

At the hotel, David woke from a very pleasant rest and saw that it was half past five. He looked around and couldn't see Eve. She must still be sunbathing. He got up and went into the bathroom to take a shower. At that moment, he wasn't worried about his new wife at all.

However, when he came out of the bathroom and she still wasn't there, he started to wonder where she had got to. It would be dark soon, so she wouldn't be able to sunbathe. Perhaps she was having a drink with Kate.

David dressed quickly and went to look for Eve. She wasn't in the bar or by the pool. He even looked in the restaurant — not that he expected her to be there. He finally knocked at James and Kate's door. Kate answered.

'You haven't seen Eve, have you?' he asked. 'She seems to have gone missing.'

'No, I haven't seen her since breakfast,' Kate replied. 'Have you looked everywhere? Silly me. Of course you must have done.'

'Yes, I have. I don't know what could have happened to her. Where can she be?'

'I think perhaps you should tell Gary.'

'I suppose so, but he and Eve don't get on, so he may be reluctant to do anything.'

'Perhaps, but it is part of his job to look after his customers.'

'Yes, I suppose you're right, though Gary did threaten Eve.'

'I'm sure that was just bravado. Look,

I'll go with you if you like.'

'Thank you, I would appreciate it. Perhaps Gary might take some notice if I come with another person.'

Kate told James what she was going to do and then they walked towards Gary's room.

'To tell you the truth, I'm a bit worried that Gary might have done something to Eve,' David confided in Kate.

She put a reassuring arm around him, not really knowing what to say. If Gary was involved in hunting, he probably didn't have any scruples and David was right to feel anxious.

After a couple of knocks, Gary finally answered the door.

'Yes?' He spoke abruptly.

Kate thought how rude he was, but they had no choice but to tell him about Eve.

'Eve's missing,' David said simply.

'Nonsense,' Gary said, making David's blood boil. How could Gary just not believe him? They weren't in a place where anyone would wander off by themselves. Eve was hardly likely to go sightseeing on her own. How dare Gary speak to him like this?

'I've looked everywhere. Do you not understand what I am saying?' David spoke sharply. 'She wouldn't leave the hotel on her own.'

'OK, OK,' Gary said. 'When did you last see her?'

'At the end of the tour. She went to sunbathe and I went to our room to have a lie down.'

'She could have gone for a walk.'

'Of course she wouldn't have done. She's not going to walk around a strange city on her own. It's not the safest of places.'

'What do you want me to do?' Gary asked.

'Ring the police.'

'They probably won't be interested. I mean, she's hardly been gone for long enough.'

'Well, make them interested. You're running a holiday company so you should have some concern for her.' David turned to walk away.

Kate followed him, amazed to hear him speak with so much passion. Eve was always the one who had something to say, not David.

'Well, Gary wasn't very helpful, was he?'

Kate was at a loss what to say. Secretly she did wonder if Gary had done something to Eve — it would certainly explain his strange reaction — but she wasn't going to say anything to upset David even more.

'No, he wasn't helpful. He's made me so angry. The police may have to wait twenty-four hours in a missing person's case, but this is different. We're in a foreign country for a start — and then we're not even supposed to be here in twenty-four hours' time. We are scheduled to be back in Mombasa by then.'

★   ★   ★

In the hospital, Abasi and Bayana, the two police officers, headed straight for Richard's ward. He lay looking very pale and drowsy, with his leg still elevated. They wondered if they would be able to get any sense out of him.

'Mr Blair, are you able to speak to us?'

Richard nodded.

'The doctor has told me that you were poisoned,' Abasi said. 'Have you got any idea who would want to kill you?'

'Yes,' Richard replied. 'It was probably the person who killed Lawrence Brady. He or she wants me dead. I don't know why, but whoever it is framed me for the murder of Lawrence and has now tried to kill me before I can prove my innocence.'

Richard coughed and there was blood. He apologised and fumbled for a tissue.

'Side effects of the poison,' he stated.

'So you are still saying you didn't kill Mr Brady.'

'Of course I didn't. Isn't it obvious?'

'There is a possibility now that you weren't the one who murdered Mr Brady,' Abasi conceded. 'Tell us, who came and gave you the injection?'

'I don't know, although there was something familiar about him. I feel as if I've seen him somewhere before. At one of the lodges perhaps. He was dressed in a nurse's uniform, so I didn't really take much notice. What's going to happen with the case?'

'We will be questioning everyone again.'

'What good will that do? Nobody is going to admit killing Lawrence or trying to kill me.'

'No, but they might slip up. Don't you worry, Mr Blair. We'll get to the bottom of this. For the time being, we are going to leave you. We will let you know what the next step will be.'

Richard lay back on his bed, exhausted. All he could think about was getting out of the hospital and back home.

Yes, he felt terrible, but this was the best thing that could have happened to him. The police would now have to reconsider their decision to arrest him for the murder of Lawrence Brady.

23

As Abasi and Bayana drove away from the hospital, Abasi's phone rang. He answered it, but he didn't say much apart from yes and no. When he closed the call, he spoke to Bayana.

'One of the women on the tour has gone missing — Eve Masters, the one who has an opinion about everything.'

'She could have just gone out.'

'She could, but she didn't tell her husband and it doesn't seem likely that she would wander off into the city on her own. With everything else that seems to be happening, she could have been abducted.'

'Why do you think that, sir?'

'She might have found something out. She is very abrupt and she could have annoyed the wrong person. This case is not as straightforward as it seems. I am no longer sure that Richard

Blair killed Mr Brady.

'For all we know, the Masters woman might have found out who the real killer is, and he or she could have killed her. If not, she could still be in serious danger.' He frowned. 'Let's get to the hotel quickly and find out what the rest of the group know.'

Bayana put his foot down on the accelerator and they sped off towards the hotel.

* * *

David was sitting in the lobby with Kate and James when the police arrived. He jumped up straight away.

'Something has happened to my wife. She wouldn't leave the hotel without telling me. She knows that it's not safe to wander around Dar es Salaam on her own.'

'Stay calm, Mr Baker. We will find her, don't worry,' Abasi said.

'How will you do that? She could be anywhere. I think you should speak to our tour guide, Gary. Eve fell out with him when she found out that he was running a hunting business. For all we know, he could have kidnapped her.'

In his distress, David spoke unguardedly, not noticing that Gary was standing near the reception desk. He glared at David.

'That isn't a reason for him to kidnap her. His business is legal,' Abasi said.

'That doesn't matter. When she found out he was also running a hunting business, she told the rest of the group, which didn't go down well, and then she started an online petition against him. It's getting a lot of signatures, so Gary may be worried that he will lose his business.'

'Yes,' Gary growled. 'I'm now getting death threats on Twitter and Facebook, even though I never talk about my hunting business on either.'

Abasi turned round.

'Well, Mr Brown, that makes you a prime suspect in the disappearance of Eve Masters.'

'Perhaps, but I have an alibi. I was with Sophie Blair all afternoon.'

'You and Sophie? What's going on?' Kate asked incredulously.

'Why shouldn't something happen between us? She says her marriage has finished.'

'You were all over Karen just yesterday,' David interrupted angrily. To him, Gary was a man with no morals or principles.

'Well, Karen wasn't interested in me any more when she found out about the hunting business. Anyway, what has this got to do with you, officers?' Gary said, ignoring David.

'Someone tried to kill Mr Blair this afternoon with rat poison,' Abasi revealed.

'He's still alive?' Gary asked.

'You sound surprised, sir,' Bayana said.

'I'm only surprised that he survived as rat poison is very dangerous. I didn't do it. As I said, I have an alibi.'

'Yes, your girlfriend, who is also the

wife of the man who has just escaped death. We will need to talk to Sophie Blair.'

'What about Eve?' David asked impatiently.

He was getting more and more frustrated. Eve was missing, but the police seemed more interested in Richard Blair's poisoning. Of course, he told himself, the two could be connected and the police might be trying to work out both crimes at the same time.

'We won't be long dealing with this matter, sir. Just wait here.'

David nodded and sat down, though not for long. He was too nervous to sit still.

* * *

'Poor Richard,' Sophie said after the police had told her what happened. 'Who could possibly have wanted to kill him?'

'You feel sympathy for this man even

though you are deserting him?' Abasi asked.

'Of course I do. I don't want anything bad to happen to him. I did love him once, after all.'

'So where were you all afternoon?'

'Here, with Gary. We were together the whole time, mostly sitting by the swimming pool.'

'What is going on between you two?'

'Nothing really. We are just starting to get to know each other.'

'So you are not having an affair?'

'Of course not,' Sophie exclaimed.

'There is one other thing. Eve Masters has disappeared.'

'Really? Well, I have had nothing to do with that. Why on earth would I want to do anything to Eve? We've become good friends.'

Abasi noticed Sophie seemed more confident than before. Had she just been pretending she was a scared tourist? Perhaps she was hiding something. Perhaps Gary was, too. Having interviewed them both, it seemed likely that Gary and Sophie were involved in one or both crimes.

Abasi called Gary over next.

'Both of you will have to stay here for the time being.'

'The tour is supposed to be going to Mombasa tomorrow morning,' Gary said.

'Nobody will be going to Mombasa, I'm afraid. We need to speak to everyone in the group again.'

'They're not going to like it,' Gary said.

'That is not my problem,' Abasi replied. 'Someone killed Lawrence Brady, tried to kill Richard Blair, and Eve Masters has disappeared. I think that this is enough to keep people here, don't you?'

Gary reluctantly nodded.

★　★　★

David paced the lobby. He just couldn't keep still. He needed to talk to the police again to see what they were going to do. Unfortunately, he didn't think there was much they could do. How were they going to find Eve in such a big city — that is, if she was still there? She could have been taken out into the bush and he dreaded to think what could happen to her there.

At last, Abasi and Bayana appeared.

'Well?' he asked. 'Any luck with those two?'

'They are of course denying any involvement. I've asked Gary to gather the group together as we need to talk to everyone.'

'How will that help to find Eve?'

'I don't know,' Abasi said. 'It will be difficult to find her. What we need is a ransom note. That is our only hope of getting your wife back.'

David raked a hand through his hair. How was he going to pay a ransom? Eve was the one with all the money. He wasn't broke, but there probably wasn't enough to pay off the people holding Eve.

Then there was the alternative

scenario. Perhaps Gary had taken Eve to dispose of her, without even thinking of a ransom. If he had wanted to get rid of her, there wasn't much anyone could do about it.

David's thoughts were interrupted by the others all coming in to the lobby. Abasi told them to sit and then informed them of Eve's disappearance and the attempted murder of Richard Blair.

'I'm afraid that I can't let you go to Mombasa tomorrow. You are all suspects.'

Joyce gasped, but Joan spoke out as usual.

'This is abominable. I shall put in a complaint.'

'Who to?' Gary asked.

Joan didn't know how to answer this, but it didn't stop her from carrying on.

'This whole holiday has been a disaster from start to finish.'

'I don't think your husband would agree, Mrs Ferguson.'

Ken just shrugged.

'Why don't you all just shut up?' David shouted, in a rare display of emotion. 'My wife is missing and all you can talk about is how awful your holiday has been.'

Everybody became quiet, even Joan.

After a pause, Abasi spoke again.

'We hope not to keep you long, but we will need to question all of you.'

Joan sighed, but didn't say anything else. David sat down. He thought bleakly that there was no hope of finding Eve — either dead or alive.

24

Despite her fear, Eve had fallen asleep. She was exhausted. She had shouted and banged on the door and on the windows, but nobody had come to her aid.

She thought that if Hamisi came back, she could try to make a run for it, but he looked strong and he did have a gun. She'd probably be caught and Hamisi would hurt or even kill her. She couldn't imagine that anyone working for Gary had scruples.

A couple of hours later, Eve stirred as she heard somebody open the padlock. She sat up and Hamisi came in.

'Some food,' he said, throwing a sandwich in a packet onto the table.

'What's the point if you're going to kill me?'

'My boss hasn't decided what to do with you.'

'Gary, you mean?'

'I don't think you need to know that.'

'I think I already know who your boss is.'

Hamisi turned to go and it was then that Eve noticed a piece of wood standing against the wall. This could be her chance. Quietly she picked it up and then, just as Hamisi was going out of the door, she hit him on the head with it. He turned to look at her and as she was going to hit him again, he grabbed the piece of wood and then her.

He threw Eve on to the floor. She tried to get up, but she couldn't. She was angry with herself. Why hadn't she hit Hamisi more powerfully? Now what was he going to do? Kill her?

Perhaps she should have waited and not been so foolish as to try and escape. Maybe Gary was just trying to frighten her and hadn't planned to do anything else to her. Now he would be angry and he could retaliate in any number of ways.

Hamisi pulled a piece of rope out of his pocket.

'I hoped not to do this, but Gary said you were a slippery character.'

Eve felt a grim satisfaction. She had been right; it was Gary who had arranged this kidnapping. How did he expect to get away with it? Everybody knew that they'd had arguments.

Perhaps it didn't matter, not if Gary could kill her and dispose of her body without anyone finding her. Maybe he would feed her to the wild animals and then there would be no proof.

Hamisi dragged Eve up on to the chair and tied up her feet and hands.

'You can stay there. I don't think the boss is going to be happy that you tried to escape. I expect that he will want to punish you. As if a little bit of wood would knock me out. Ha.'

'You've admitted that your boss is Gary, so I know everything now.'

'What good will it do you? I doubt if you'll be alive for long enough to tell anybody about it.'

With that Hamisi left, locking the door behind him. Eve felt tears starting to fall. What a mess. All she had really done was stand up for animal rights, and look where that had got her. How was she going to get out of this situation? For the first time in her life, she felt bereft of all hope.

★ ★ ★

Everybody in the group was questioned, but Abasi and Bayana left soon afterwards. It seemed as if nobody had anything constructive to say concerning the disappearance of Eve.

David couldn't face dinner, not without his wife, but he was too restless to stay in his room. He wanted to go out and find her, but where would he start? He decided to go to the bar and have a drink to try and calm his nerves, even though he knew it wouldn't do much good.

After downing a double whisky, David went to the lobby to wait.

Perhaps Eve might come back and he wanted to be there to greet her.

Although the police had left, Abasi had given David his personal number in case Eve contacted him or he heard anything.

He sat down trying to calm his frayed nerves, but all he could think about was Eve. He remembered their wedding, thinking how perfect it had been. He hadn't wanted a big wedding, but he knew Eve did, so he had agreed to it. In the end, even he had thought that getting married on the beach was both magical and romantic.

'How are you holding up, David?' Kate's voice shook him out of his memories.

'Kate, James, I'm not doing so well. Eve has got into trouble before, but this is worse. Nobody has any idea where she is and it's such a big city. Even if she escaped from wherever she is, she might not be able to get back here.'

'I'm sure it will be all right, David. Eve's told me how she's escaped from similar situations,' Kate replied. 'She's a tough cookie. She'll be fine.'

David tried to smile, but it was a struggle. Eve wasn't in her comfort zone here, and he started imagining the worst.

'Why don't you come and have a drink in the bar, David?' James asked.

'No, not at the moment,' David replied. 'You go ahead and I'll join you in a little while.'

James and Kate left reluctantly, although they had no idea how to help David.

David sat there in the shadows for a few moments, wishing he knew what to do. Then he saw Gary talking to Hamisi. He was convinced that they were involved in Eve's disappearance.

Gary started to walk towards the front door of the hotel, while Hamisi disappeared into the restaurant. David was sure neither of them had seen him sitting there. He had a split second to decide what to do. He got up slowly and followed Gary out of the hotel. He had no idea if Gary was going to see Eve, but it was his only shot.

He saw Gary get into a taxi and he jumped into the one behind it.

'Follow that cab,' he said urgently. 'But please keep your distance.'

'You're the boss,' the cab driver said as he put his car into gear.

★ ★ ★

David sat shaking in the cab. He had to do this, but he also had to admit that he was frightened. Gary was a dangerous man and he had to keep his wits about him if he wanted to find Eve. He wondered how Eve had been able to chase criminals back on Crete without being scared witless. He suddenly realised that he was married to a very strong woman.

Gary's cab was travelling fast and David was worried that he might realise that he was being followed. However, David's cab driver was keeping far away enough from them not to be noticed, and there were plenty of other cars on both sides of the road. David hoped that they wouldn't be spotted.

They hadn't gone far when Gary's cab started to slow down. David wondered if his driver had done something like this before as he maintained a discreet distance, finally stopping behind another car.

'Can you wait here?' David asked.

'I'm not going anywhere before I'm paid.'

David took this to mean that he would wait for him. He decided not to even leave a deposit otherwise the taxi might go away.

Gary had got out of his cab and had started walking towards a derelict building. David got out and crept along behind him at what he thought was a safe distance. There were other people around and he hoped he had become part of the crowd. He was still shaking. Perhaps Eve had been in these sorts of situations before, but he hadn't, and he felt out of his depth. However, he had to rescue her and he was pretty certain that Gary was going to see her.

Gary stopped at a door and started fiddling in his pocket. David thought he was looking for the key and it wasn't long before he found what he wanted. Luckily he didn't turn around but just put the key in the door. It opened and Gary went in, leaving it ajar as was his habit.

David hovered close by, listening intently.

'Well, Ms Masters, what are we going to do with you?' he heard Gary say.

'Just let me go and I won't tell anyone that you had me kidnapped,' Eve replied.

'Do you really expect me to believe that, Ms Masters, or may I call you Eve?'

Gary suddenly erupted into laughter. Both Eve and David thought that he had totally lost the plot.

'Look, Gary,' Eve said. 'I'll be gone soon so you don't have to worry about me. What can I do from my quiet home in Greece anyway?'

'You can do plenty of damage from your computer, Ms Masters, wherever you are. I can do without negative publicity.'

'Well, you deserve it,' Eve said. She wasn't going to die a coward. She was going to say exactly what she felt and believed in.

'You are certainly very cocky for someone who's tied up and at my mercy.'

'You will do whatever you want to do and I'm not going to go out simpering and shaking.'

'Really, Ms Masters?' Gary said, grinning as he reached into his pocket.

At that moment David, who had been hiding just behind the door, lunged at Gary, bringing him down. Eve couldn't believe her eyes. There was a tussle, but that piece of wood was just within David's reach. He grabbed it and hit Gary — hard — on the head.

★   ★   ★

As soon as David had untied the ropes, Eve flung her arms around him.

'I can't believe you're here. How on earth did you find me?'

'I followed Gary in a taxi. I thought it was my only chance to find you. Oh, Eve, I was so worried. I really thought that I had lost you.'

David put his lips on Eve's and she kissed him with such passion that he dissolved into the moment, forgetting for a split second where they were. Eve knew she was lucky to have him. This time she had really thought that it was all over.

'Come on, we'd better get going before Gary wakes up,' David said, pulling away. There would be plenty of time for romance later.

'How are we going to get away from here, darling?'

'I have a taxi waiting. I didn't pay him, so I'm sure he'll still be there.'

As David expected, his taxi was waiting — but so was Gary's.

'We'd better be quick,' David said.

'Gary's taxi driver might go and see where he is and could call the police. We need to see them before he does.'

Eve and David got into the taxi and he told the driver to get back to their hotel as quickly as possible.

'What happened?' David asked Eve as they travelled back to the hotel. 'How did you end up here, in what seems to be a very seedy area?'

'Hamisi hit me on the head in the lift at the hotel. I was coming back to our room after sunbathing. When I woke up, I was in a place I didn't recognise. I mean, how far are we from the hotel?'

'We're pretty close, Eve.'

'I thought he might have taken me to the bush and I could have been eaten by wild animals.'

'Oh Eve, you do have an overactive imagination, but then I suppose they could have done anything to you. It doesn't bear thinking about.'

'You really are my hero, David. I didn't know how I was going to get out of this one. I suppose you're cross with me for interfering?'

'No, not this time. All you did was write out a petition. That doesn't deserve kidnapping.'

Eve smiled weakly. She decided not to tell David about her interest in Lawrence Brady's case. Why disturb the peace?

★ ★ ★

As the cab sped towards the hotel, David phoned Abasi. After he explained what had happened, Abasi told him they weren't far from the hotel and would soon be there.

'But what about Gary?' Eve asked. 'The police need to pick him up otherwise I'll never be safe.'

'Do you know the address of where we've just been?' Gary asked the taxi driver.

'Yes, I can write it down for you when we stop.'

'Thank goodness,' Eve said, relieved.

'As long as Gary doesn't wake up and try to escape.'

'There is always that possibility, but we'll have to hope that I well and truly knocked him out.'

Eve sighed. What were the chances that he wouldn't wake up? His taxi was still there so he could get away. Why hadn't the police suggested picking him up first? Why hadn't she or David thought of suggesting it? All she could think about now was how incompetent the police here were.

★   ★   ★

In minutes, Eve and David were back at the hotel. David tipped the driver generously for his helpfulness. They both rushed in to find Abasi and Bayana already there.

'We've got the address of the place I was kept,' Eve exclaimed. 'You have to go and pick up Gary.'

'Don't worry. He won't get far,' Abasi replied.

'Here's the address,' David said, shoving the paper into Abasi's hand. He too was feeling that police methods here left a lot to be desired.

'I'll get my men to go and pick Gary up.'

Abasi took out his phone and made a quick call.

'Mrs Masters, you are not hurt?' he asked.

'No, I'm fine.'

'So Gary Brown abducted you?'

'Not exactly; a man called Hamisi hit me over the head and took me to the place where Gary is now. I'm certain that he works for Gary. I saw them together at Taita Hills when Gary apparently threatened to kill someone. Then Hamisi kept appearing at all the lodges we stayed at, but he didn't travel with us. Then Gary turned up at the shack, so I knew it was him who had arranged to have me kidnapped.'

'You didn't tell us that Gary had threatened to kill someone. Why not?'

'I'm sorry, but I thought it was

someone who worked for him. I didn't think it had anything to do with Lawrence Brady.'

'You should still have told us. Did Gary know you overheard him?'

'I'm pretty sure he didn't.'

'Gary is under the impression that you are trying to destroy his hunting business,' Abasi continued. 'Do you think that is why you were kidnapped?'

'I would imagine so. I think he wanted to teach me a lesson — or maybe he did want to get rid of me.'

Eve shivered. What a honeymoon this was turning out to be. It wouldn't be a surprise if David left her, unable to take any more.

'Perhaps Gary was going to send a ransom note?'

'I hardly think so,' Eve replied, thinking that the police really didn't have a clue. All Gary wanted was to punish her.

'Who knows what has been going on in his head?' Abasi continued.

'Don't you think you should go and

find Hamisi?' Eve said. 'He's probably in the hotel somewhere.'

'I think we know how to do our job,' Abasi replied reprovingly.

Eve shook her head. She didn't feel at all confident that they knew what they were doing.

★   ★   ★

Abasi and Bayana found out which room Hamisi was in. There was no reply, even when they knocked again. They then went to the bar and the restaurant, but he was nowhere to be found. Finally they went to the desk and asked for the spare key to Hamisi's room. The desk clerk was reluctant to give it to them.

'I don't think I'm allowed to do that,' she said nervously.

'We are the police and the man is under suspicion for kidnapping. We have every right to go in to his room.'

She reluctantly handed the key over and the two police officers dashed back to Hamisi's room. As they entered, they saw Hamisi packing his case. Both Abasi and Bayana drew out their guns and Hamisi went for his.

'Don't even try, Hamisi.' Abasi let a bullet fly into the wall. 'The next bullet will be yours.'

Hamisi put his hands in the air and Bayana went over and cuffed him.

'We'll make this easy on you, Hamisi,' Abasi said. 'We know that Gary Brown told you to kidnap Mrs Masters. It's better if you admit what you did. You were acting under Gary's orders and you'll get a lighter sentence if you tell us exactly what happened.'

'I didn't want to do it,' Hamisi said, sounding frightened. 'I work for Gary in his hunting business. It's all legal, whatever that woman, Masters, says. I didn't want to get involved with kidnapping her, but Gary made me.'

'How could he make you do this? You have your own mind.'

'Gary is dangerous. He has been prepared to kill other employees who

don't do what he says. He only
threatened to sack me, but I have seven
children. I make good money from
Gary. I need it to support my family.'

'How did you know Eve Masters had
escaped?'

Hamisi didn't answer.

'Come on, Hamisi. You must know
what has happened, or you wouldn't be
packing your bags.'

Hamisi paused for a moment before
answering.

'OK. Gary phoned and asked me to
meet him.'

'So he's woken up. Damn.'

'He also asked me to bring Sophie
Blair.'

'Why? It doesn't make sense.'

'I don't know. I think he has a thing
for her.'

Abasi looked shocked. He had never
thought that Gary would want to take
Sophie with him. She had said that they
were only getting to know each other.
Gary was certainly a quick worker.
Perhaps this explained why Sophie

wasn't bothered about seeing her husband again.

'Bayana, stay with Hamisi here while I search for Mrs Blair.'

Bayana nodded.

Abasi went down to the bar and saw Sophie sitting with Eve and David.

'Mrs Blair, I would like a word with you.'

'What am I supposed to have done now?'

'We know that Gary Brown has asked Hamisi to bring you to him.'

'Why would he do that? I hardly know Gary apart from as a guide. What would he want with me?'

'Come now, Mrs Blair, I think that you and he were having an affair.'

'That's a lie. I told you before that we weren't,' Sophie spoke angrily.

'Maybe not,' Eve interrupted, 'but I saw you and Gary kissing in the museum.'

Sophie only paused for a second.

'It was nothing. We had one kiss, that's all.'

'Is this why you're not bothered about seeing your husband?' Eve continued, despite Abasi glaring at her. It was his investigation, not hers.

'No, I don't love him any more — but I certainly don't love Gary Brown.'

'So Hamisi hasn't told you that Gary wants you to come with him?' Abasi asked.

'No, of course not. I mean, it's crazy. Why on earth would I go on the run with some criminal?'

'So you don't know that he instructed Hamisi to kidnap Mrs Masters?'

'Of course not.'

'Well, Mrs Blair, for the moment, don't leave the hotel. We will probably want to see you again.'

'Where on earth would I go?' Sophie responded, shaking her head.

Eve noticed Sophie was perspiring, which didn't surprise her. She seemed to be in a tight corner with no way out. She had got herself embroiled with Gary and was now part of the investigation.

However, Eve was having trouble understanding what was going on. Gary had spent most of his time on the safari with Karen. Now, after one kiss, he wanted to take Sophie away with him. It didn't sound at all logical.

Abasi's phone rang and he answered it immediately. He said very little and Eve started to worry. When he ended the call, he spoke.

'I'm afraid that Mr Brown has gone. He obviously woke up and made a run for it. My men are out looking for him.'

Abasi studied Sophie's face.

'Are you worried that he's gone without you?'

'Not at all. I wouldn't have gone with him. We had one kiss. That doesn't warrant me giving up my life and leaving with him.'

Eve stared at Sophie. She looked so full of confidence now. Had she been play-acting before?

'I'm a bit worried that Gary might come after Eve,' David said.

'I'm sure his plan will be to do a

runner,' Abasi replied.

'Yes,' Eve said. 'He might run now, but who's to say he won't come after me later, when all this has died down?'

'Mrs Masters, we plan on catching Gary before the night is out.'

Eve tried to smile, but she wasn't very convinced. Still, she'd stand up for the rights of animals again, even if it put her life in danger.

25

Not long after Eve and David had returned to the hotel, Gary had begun to stir. His head was very painful, but that was the least of his worries. All he felt was fury that Eve had managed to get away. She and that idiot of a husband of hers might have made it back to the hotel and the police could already have been called.

He shook his head. Eve's husband wasn't as stupid as he seemed. He had succeeded in overpowering him; few people had ever been able to do that.

Gary got out his phone. He had to warn Hamisi that the police might come to the hotel.

'Hamisi, get out of the hotel as soon as you can and meet me at Denny's Bar. Bring that Sophie woman with you.'

'What's happening? Why do you want Sophie?'

'I like her, OK? Eve Masters has escaped so we have to get out of the country.'

Gary ended the call quickly. He couldn't waste any more time. He had no idea how long he had been out cold. The police could be on their way already. He got up, feeling a sharp pain in his head, but he ignored it. As he stumbled outside, he saw his taxi was still there. He ran towards it and leaped in, giving instructions.

★   ★   ★

At the police station, Hamisi decided he wasn't going to say anything more until he had a lawyer present. Hopefully by that time Gary would have been caught and the police would direct their attention towards him. After all, he was the boss.

Abasi was trying to trick more information out of him. He was sure the attempt on Richard's life had something to do with Hamisi and Gary.

295

'So Gary told you to kill Richard Blair?'

Hamisi said nothing.

Abasi slammed his fist on the table.

'Say something, before you come to regret your decision to keep quiet.'

Hamisi wondered if the police might beat him up, so he decided to give them a little information to hopefully get them off his back.

'I didn't kill Mr Blair.'

'But that was the intention?'

'I'm not saying any more,' Hamisi replied.

Abasi was frustrated.

'Look, Hamisi, if you tell us the truth, you'll get a better deal. You're already going to prison, but I can make things easier for you. So, did your boss say why he wanted Mr Blair killed?'

'It wasn't Gary,' Hamisi said after a few moments. 'It was Blair's wife, Sophie, who wanted him dead. She's a rich woman and she didn't want her husband to get any of it in a nasty divorce settlement.'

Both officers looked shocked. Neither

had any idea that Sophie was behind Richard's poisoning.

'So she approached you? How did she know you?' Abasi finally continued.

'She didn't. She asked Gary for help. They hit it off as soon as they met. Love at first sight, you could say.'

'I was under the impression that Gary and Karen Lane were together,' Abasi stated.

'It was just a cover-up as far as Gary was concerned.'

'Well, thank you, Hamisi. You've been very helpful for a man who said he didn't want to speak without a lawyer.'

'I just don't want to be blamed for what others have done.'

'Don't worry — everybody who has committed a crime will be punished.'

Hamisi didn't know whether to be worried or relieved.

★   ★   ★

Eve and David decided to go to their room to freshen up before dinner.

Sophie had stayed in the bar having another drink, but as she got up, she saw Hamisi being taken away. She started to panic. Would he give her up to the police? She rushed back to her room, bumping into Eve and David. She dropped her bag and everything spilled out onto the floor.

Eve bent down to help her pick up her things.

'It's all right, I can do it myself,' Sophie snapped.

'Sorry, I was only trying to help.'

'Well don't. I don't need any help.'

'Fine,' Eve replied.

She couldn't be bothered to tell her to stop being so rude. It had been a long and tiring day.

As they entered the restaurant, Kate signalled to Eve and David.

'How are you, Eve?'

'I'm OK. A little shaken up still, but most of all, I'm starving!'

Everyone laughed before looking at their menus. As they were deciding, Karen came in. She had seen Hamisi being led away by the police and headed straight for Eve's table.

'Did you know that Gary's friend, Hamisi, has just been arrested? You were right about Gary, Eve — even more so because he went off with Sophie as soon as I had dumped him.'

'How do you know that?'

'I saw them holding hands earlier today.'

'I think he may have already been seeing Sophie, Karen. I'm sorry.'

'How do you know?'

'I saw them kissing in the museum. It didn't look like a first-time kiss.'

Eve wasn't happy telling Karen this, but felt the more that she thought that Gary was a good-for-nothing so-and-so, the better. It might then be easier for her to get over him.

'Why ever did he hook up with me, Eve? I feel such a fool.'

Karen looked as if she might burst into tears.

'You're nothing of the sort. Gary's the fool, thinking he could get away with all this. He treated you terribly, so you're not to blame.'

Karen tried to smile.

'You know,' Eve continued, 'I'm getting a bad feeling about the whole situation. Sophie was in such a hurry when we bumped into her before coming here. I need to check on her. She might be going out to see Gary. We should get the police back.'

'Eve,' David warned. 'Don't get involved. Let the police handle this the best way they can.'

'I'm only going to see if Sophie's still here. I promise I won't do anything else except ring the police if she's gone.'

Eve jumped up, not allowing David to say anything more. As she walked in to the lobby, she saw Sophie disappearing out through the front door with her suitcase. In a split second, Eve decided to run after her, and as she got outside, she saw Sophie getting into a taxi. She rushed to intercept her, but didn't quite make it. There were no more taxis so she couldn't follow her. Eve was frustrated. Why hadn't she run a bit faster?

She went back to the others.

'She's gone, taking her suitcase. I saw her getting into a taxi, but I couldn't quite catch her.'

'We should ring the police,' Kate said. 'She's probably going to meet Gary. Did she see you, Eve?'

'I don't think she did, though what difference it would have made if she had, I don't know. She's gone and we've lost the chance of finding Gary.'

'Eve, the police are competent enough to find them. I have the inspector's mobile number. Do you want to do the honours?' David asked.

He knew Eve was disappointed that she hadn't managed to stop Sophie, so he thought it would be good if she informed the police.

Eve took the phone and dialled Abasi's number.

26

Sophie was standing in a queue waiting to see if she could get a plane ticket out of the country when a hand grasped her arm.

She turned, a shiver of fear running down her spine. However she relaxed on seeing who it was.

'Gary, darling, thank goodness it's you.'

'You weren't thinking of leaving without me, were you?' Gary asked, sounding uptight.

'Of course not. Why on earth would I want to do that?'

'You're standing here trying to get a ticket. I didn't tell Hamisi to bring you here. I have a friend with a helicopter who will get us out of the country and we were supposed to meet at Denny's Bar.'

'What are you doing here then?' Sophie asked.

'I waited in the bar, but when neither you nor Hamisi turned up. I put two and two together and came here.'

'Hamisi was arrested. I didn't know what to do. I just wanted to get out of the country. I was afraid you had been arrested as well.'

Sophie looked imploringly at Gary and his heart melted. There weren't many people who could touch him, but unfortunately Sophie was one of the few who could. He knew he could be risking everything for her, but he felt that he had no choice.

'Come on then, let's go before it's too late. The police might come here first to try and catch us. They've probably warned Customs to be on the look-out for us.'

'They don't think I've done anything, do they?'

'I wouldn't be surprised if Hamisi has told them everything. He's not good under pressure.'

'Great,' Sophie snarled. 'Now we could both go to jail.'

She sounded very angry, a side of her which Gary hadn't seen before. Why was he risking everything for this woman? However, he knew he couldn't give her up.

'I'll make sure we don't go to jail, don't you worry. Come on, let's get out of here.'

Gary grabbed Sophie's suitcase and took her hand. They walked quickly towards the exit of the airport. As they came out on to the road, Gary hailed a taxi, just as Abasi and Bayana's patrol car drew up. The officers leaped out, hurrying towards the entrance.

Quickly Gary helped Sophie in to the taxi. Unfortunately for them, Abasi saw them, called over Bayana, and they jumped back into their car. Abasi put the siren on. For a while the cab didn't slow down, but then the driver spoke.

'What have you done?' he asked. 'The police are chasing us. I have to stop.'

'You'll do nothing of the kind,' Gary

said, pointing his gun at the cab driver's neck.

The driver started to tremble and found he was losing control of the car.

'Get a grip, man,' Gary said, 'or I'll take you hostage. You would be a good bargaining tool with the police.'

The driver tried to concentrate, but the police car was gaining ground. He put his foot on the accelerator and sped up, but Abasi and Bayana managed to keep up with him. He drove round tight bends, tyres screeching, but couldn't shake off the police. As he rounded one bend on the wrong side of the road, another car came towards them. He swerved, but the cars hit each other. The cab went skidding into the side of the road.

Once the car had come to rest, Sophie looked at Gary. He was out cold, and so was the cab driver. She had to get away. She didn't even think where she might go, but she wrenched the door open and set off running as fast as she could.

However, it was no good. Seconds later, she was brought to the ground. Bayana pulled her arms behind her and Abasi cuffed her.

'I haven't done anything. Let me go!' Sophie screeched.

'Why did you run, then?' Abasi asked. 'It doesn't look good.'

'I was scared, that was all.'

Sophie had gone pale and she felt sick. How was she going to get out of this?

Abasi started to move towards the car and Bayana dragged Sophie behind him. She had decided that she wasn't going to go quietly.

Abasi looked into the car. He felt the cab driver's pulse and then shook his head.

'He's gone. He didn't have a seat belt on. This is not right, Mrs Blair. He isn't the one who is guilty of any crimes.'

Then Abasi looked in the back seat and saw Gary starting to stir. His gun was on the seat beside him and Abasi seized it.

306

Gary looked up.

'We are arresting you for the abduction of Eve Masters and the murder of Lawrence Brady.'

Gary had double vision after the second blow to his head in a few hours, but he knew Abasi's voice — and he knew the game was up.

'Yes, I arranged to have that Masters woman abducted — but I didn't kill Lawrence Brady. *She* did,' he growled, pointing to Sophie.

★   ★   ★

In the police station, Gary sat in front of Abasi and Bayana. He had a bump on his forehead as well as one on the back of his skull from the blow David had given him. They hurt like hell, but the police officers had refused him any pain killers.

'I'll speak to my lawyer about this,' Gary said angrily.

He wasn't intimidated by the police officers. He had been in this sort of situation before and had always got out of it. Yes, he might get blamed for the kidnapping of Eve Masters, but he wasn't going to take the rap for Lawrence Brady's murder.

'So, Mr Brown, why did you have Eve Masters abducted? There's no point denying it. Hamisi has already told us that it was your plan. After all, he had no reason to do this off his own back.'

'I only wanted to frighten her. She was trying to destroy my hunting business. I wasn't planning to kill her.'

Abasi's eyes met his suspect's. All he could see was pure evil, and he had no idea if he believed him. Unfortunately he wouldn't get as long a sentence for abduction as for murder.

Abasi didn't like this man. He didn't support hunting and could understand Eve's loathing of the so-called sport.

'What did you plan to do with her, then?'

'I would have let her go and then started a new hunting business elsewhere. There are plenty of countries in

Africa to choose from.'

'What about your holiday business?'

'I'm finding it rather dull. I was going to let my partner buy me out.'

Abasi was getting frustrated. Gary had an answer for everything and he never hesitated when replying.

'So, what about Lawrence Brady? You say you didn't kill him; Sophie did. How do you expect us to believe you?'

'She told me. It's as simple as that.'

'Why? Why did Sophie Blair kill a man she had previously had an affair with?'

'It was more than an affair. They were going to be married. He wouldn't accept her rejection and wouldn't leave her alone. He found out that she was going on this safari and followed her. He pretended to be interested in Karen Lane in the hope of making Sophie jealous. However, she saw through him and decided he had to go.'

'Murder seems an extreme reaction.'

'She didn't think she could get rid of him any other way.'

'She's not a big woman. How could she have overpowered him?'

'Easy. She surprised him while he was asleep.'

'I suppose the next thing you'll be saying is that she tried to kill her husband, Richard Blair.'

'Physically no. She employed Hamisi to do it.'

'Why? Isn't divorce a better option?'

'She's a wealthy woman. She didn't want Richard getting any of her money.'

Abasi shook his head. Was Gary telling the truth?

'You also have a motive to kill Brady. After all, he was a reporter. He could have exposed you.'

'He would need more information to make a good story. Photos would have been helpful and it would be difficult to get any. He had nothing apart from the fact that I run a hunting business.'

'And you and Sophie? This seems a whirlwind romance.'

'Not really. We met in England when I was last there. It was love at first sight, so to speak. Her husband had always wanted to go on safari so she arranged it. She wanted to see if she could live here.'

'And could she?'

'Yes, of course. She pretended to hate it, but she doesn't, nor does she care one way or another about my hunting business.'

'Your story is pretty incredible, Mr Brown. Why should we believe you?'

'Because it's the truth, though I expect you'll make your own minds up about that.'

'Very well, Mr Brown. I think that will be all for now. You will be put in a cell for the time being.'

Gary shrugged. It wouldn't be the first time. Anyway, he had an excellent lawyer and should be able to get away from this with just a short sentence for the abduction of Eve Masters. He was sorry that Sophie was going to have to go to jail for years. She was beautiful and he was in love with her. However, rather her than him in jail.

Sophie sat in front of the police officers. She seemed quite calm and Abasi was filled with a sense of trepidation. This woman was as cool as a cucumber.

Perhaps Gary had been telling the truth. If she was innocent, she would probably be more scared. Was she a psychopath?

'We have information that you killed Mr Lawrence Brady,' Abasi said.

'Who told you that?' She laughed. 'I suppose that it was that idiot of a man, Gary Brown.'

'An idiot? You were running off with him.'

'He forced me to.'

'Now why would he do that?'

'Because he's crazy about me.'

Throughout the exchange, she didn't lose her cool.

'I'll put it this way, Mrs Blair; you killed Mr Brady because he wouldn't leave you alone and then you attempted to kill your husband so that he doesn't get anything out of you financially.'

'I did not touch Richard.'

'No, you paid Hamisi to kill him, but he didn't succeed. Hamisi has already admitted this so it will be your word against his.'

'I think a jury would be more likely to believe me rather than Hamisi.'

'Not if they know all the facts.'

'I have nothing else to say,' Sophie said.

Abasi and Bayana looked at each other. This case was getting more complicated by the minute. They decided to send Sophie back to her cell and start interrogating her again the following day.

* * *

Abasi and Bayana were just ready to call it a night when a phone call came through. It was from Richard Blair at the hospital. He wanted to see them. Abasi asked if it could be the following day, but he insisted that it was important.

'Mr Blair, what can we do for you?' he asked as they strode into his room.

Richard wondered if he was imagining the fact that they were being less sharp with him.

'I have something to tell you about the murder of Lawrence Brady. It was my wife, Sophie, who killed him — not me.'

'Really,' Abasi responded. 'Why have you not told us this before?'

'Because I loved her. I still love her, but she has told me that our marriage is over. Why should I be punished for something I didn't do?'

'So how do you know she killed Mr Brady?'

'I woke up early on the morning he was killed. I saw Sophie creep out of bed and leave. I followed her; she went to Lawrence's room. I thought of confronting them, but decided against it. If she was having an affair with that man, I didn't want to know. I decided to try and be a better husband.

'When I heard Lawrence had been murdered, I knew it was Sophie and I was glad. She had chosen me over him, so I didn't say anything.

'However, when she told me she wanted a divorce a couple of days ago, I couldn't believe it. I didn't know what to do. I still love her, you see. Even so, I've come to accept that she doesn't love me, so why should I go to jail for her?'

Bayana had been taking notes and Abasi asked Richard if he would sign a statement.

'Yes, of course,' Richard replied.

Abasi noticed a tinge of regret in his voice, but it was understandable. He had lost the woman he loved; it wasn't an easy thing for a man to bear.

★   ★   ★

Bayana was all set to go home after this interview, but Abasi had other ideas.

'Come on. Back to the police station to question Mrs Blair again.'

315

'What, now? Can't it wait until the morning?'

'No, it can't,' Abasi snapped. 'I want this business done and dusted tonight.'

Bayana reluctantly drove them both back to the police station, and it wasn't long before Sophie was sitting in front of the two officers again.

'What on earth is this all about?' Sophie asked petulantly. 'I was just falling asleep.'

She didn't sound at all afraid.

'Someone has come forward to say that they saw you going into Mr Brady's room early in the morning on the day he was killed.'

'Who told you this?' she asked.

Abasi noticed a slight tremor in her voice. For the first time, she sounded a little afraid.

'It doesn't matter who, but this person has given us a signed statement. This, with Gary Brown's evidence, leaves us in no doubt that you murdered Lawrence Brady.'

For a moment Sophie looked as if

she might burst into tears, but she then sat up straight, looking composed.

'OK, I know when I'm beaten. I did kill him, but for the record, it was in self-defence. Lawrence wouldn't let me go. We'd had a relationship, but he couldn't understand that it was over. He found out that I was going on this trip and followed me.

'I went to his room early that morning to try to reason with him. It didn't work. He grabbed me and I thought he was going to kill me. That's when I saw his penknife on the bedside table. I grabbed it and stabbed him in the stomach. He fell on the bed and that's when I slashed his throat. It was pure self defence.'

'That's not what it sounds like to me. You could have let it be when you stabbed him in the stomach, but you didn't. You went one step further and made sure he was dead. Then you let your husband be blamed for his murder.'

'What was I going to do? Admit

murdering Lawrence when there was someone else you suspected? Richard made it easy when he ran away from you in the Serengeti.'

'Yes, we were sure he was the murderer.'

'I suppose he'll go free now?' Sophie sighed.

'Yes, of course he will. By the way, what did you do with the penknife?'

'I threw it out of the window on a game drive when no one was looking. You really should have searched us.' She smirked.

Abasi was becoming angry. This woman wasn't afraid of him and he didn't like it. She should be scared witless as she had a long jail sentence in front of her.

'Back to your cell,' Abasi said. 'This interview is over.'

As Sophie got up, she smiled as if she didn't care about anything. Abasi thought she would definitely need to see a psychiatrist.

27

Eve hardly slept. The whole business was going round and round in her head and she couldn't get Sophie out of her mind.

How deep was she in all this? That woman confused Eve. She had seemed weak, but she was nothing of the sort. Even if she hadn't murdered anyone, and Eve wasn't at all sure about that, she was a part of the whole situation.

Eve urgently wanted to know all the facts. She felt that she had been out of her depth in this case and she didn't like it. She actually longed for Crete and her sparring exchanges with detective chief inspector Dimitris Kastrinakis. She had always managed to stay one step in front of him. Was this the end of her career as a self-appointed private eye?

At least Gary should go to jail for

having her kidnapped, but unfortunately it probably wouldn't be the end
of his hunting business. She resolved to
do more in the fight against hunting
when she got back to Crete. In
particular, she was going to follow
Gary's career as closely as she could.

Then Eve's mind drifted back to the
few hours she had spent locked up. She
had been frightened; there was no
doubt about it. Yes, this had happened
to her before, but she had always felt a
sense of control on Crete. Here, she
didn't.

Had they really planned to kill her?
She could have been anywhere, even
out in the bush, but she had been lucky,
so very lucky. Then of course, there was
her beloved David. He had been
extremely brave following Gary. If it
hadn't been for him she could still be
locked up, or worse.

It was the early hours of the morning
when Eve finally got to sleep.

★　★　★

The following morning, the members of the group were all having breakfast when the police officer, Abasi, arrived. He asked them to come to the lobby when they had finished their meal.

'I hope they're not going to keep us here much longer,' Joan grumbled. 'The sooner I'm out of this country, the better.'

Eve was going to reply, but thought better of it. Joan moaned the whole time, so nothing would satisfy her. She wasn't worth the bother. Instead, Eve tucked into her scrambled eggs, hoping that Abasi would tell them exactly what was going on.

When they all arrived in the lobby, the chief inspector was very brief and told them Gary wouldn't be carrying on with the trip and that Adhama would drive them to Mombasa in about an hour's time. Everyone apart from Eve seemed satisfied.

She jumped up as Abasi was leaving and cornered him. David hoped she wasn't going to annoy him with too many questions. He knew she wanted answers and while he wished that she wasn't interfering again, David too was interested to find out who had been arrested and for what.

'Sir,' Eve said, trying to be as polite as possible. 'Can you tell me what's happened? I was part of it after all, wasn't I?'

'Very well. I suppose you deserve to hear the truth. Sophie Blair has been arrested for the murder of Lawrence Brady. She admitted killing him, saying that he wouldn't leave her alone and wanted their relationship to continue. She was also the one who hired Hamisi to kill Richard as she didn't want to give him any money in the divorce settlement. Finally, although Hamisi kidnapped you, Gary was behind the plot. Satisfied?'

Eve was stunned. However, she wasn't totally surprised that Sophie was a murderer. She had seemed so weak, but that was probably all a cover-up. At times Sophie had seemed as hard as nails; that must have been her true personality.

'Thank you for letting me know. I had a hard time sleeping last night.'

'Don't worry, Mrs Masters, all three of them will be behind bars for a long time to come.'

'Oh — there is one other thing. Did you find out who it was that vandalised Joan and Ken's room?'

'We discovered that it was a girl who worked at the lodge who is very anti-hunting.'

'Good for her,' Eve said, smiling.

'Not really. She's been sacked and will go to prison for a short time.'

Eve shook her head. That was certainly unfair, although she wasn't surprised. In her mind, the girl should be praised for doing what she did.

Eve went back to David and told him what Abasi had said. He was also amazed that Sophie was a killer, although he agreed that there was something suspicious about her.

'The sooner we get to Mombasa and

relax, the better,' he said. 'This honeymoon hasn't quite turned out as it should have done.'

'I'm sorry, David.'

'Don't be, darling. For once you didn't get too involved. I blame Gary, not you.'

Eve threw her arms around her husband.

'I don't know how I managed before I met you, David. I do love you.'

'I love you too. Now let's go and enjoy the rest of our honeymoon.'

★ ★ ★

Two days later, Eve and David were sitting by the swimming pool at their hotel in Mombasa. They sipped margaritas, not saying much, but occasionally smiling at each other. At last they felt relaxed after the trauma of the past few days.

The setting was beautiful, with views of the clear blue Indian Ocean and long sandy beaches. Eve thought how lucky she was to be here with David. It could easily have turned out so differently.

All of a sudden, she put down her drink and bent over to David, kissing him gently.

'Thank you for being such a wonderful husband.'

'Thank you for being a fantastic wife.'

'Even after what we've been through? It should all have been so different.'

'None of it was really your fault, so let's put it behind us.'

'OK. I never thought I would say this, but I'm actually looking forward to getting back to Crete. I think I'm finally beginning to think of it as home.'

'I'm so happy you think that at last,' David said, taking Eve's hand.

Eve leaned back and smiled. Yes, the quiet life was all she wanted from now on.

She didn't realise there was a man watching them until his mobile rang.

'Mr Neil Brown. Your flight to Chania, Crete, in five days is confirmed. Have a good vacation.'

'Thank you. I'm sure I will,' he replied, smiling.

We do hope that you have enjoyed reading this large print book.

Did you know that all of our titles are available for purchase?

We publish a wide range of high quality large print books including:
Romances, Mysteries, Classics
General Fiction
Non Fiction and Westerns

Special interest titles available in large print are:
The Little Oxford Dictionary
Music Book, Song Book
Hymn Book, Service Book

Also available from us courtesy of Oxford University Press:
Young Readers' Dictionary
(large print edition)
Young Readers' Thesaurus
(large print edition)

For further information or a free brochure, please contact us at:
Ulverscroft Large Print Books Ltd.,
The Green, Bradgate Road, Anstey,
Leicester, LE7 7FU, England.
Tel: (00 44) **0116 236 4325**
Fax: (00 44) **0116 234 0205**

HERE COMES THE BEST MAN

Angela Britnell

When troubled army veteran and musician Josh Robertson returns home to Nashville to be the best man at his younger brother Chad's wedding, he's sure that he's going to mess it all up somehow. But when it becomes clear that the wedding might not be going to plan, it's up to him and fellow guest Louise Giles to save the day. Can Josh be the best man his brother needs? And is there somebody else who is beginning to realise that Josh could be her 'best man' too?

FARMER WANTS A WIFE

Sarah Purdue

Skye works in London, with no intention of ever going back to the farming life in which she was raised. Then she travels to meet with Charles, a new client who lives in rural Wales. When she crashes her car in heavy snow, she is rescued by Ren and Gethin. Snowbound, she starts helping on their farm — and growing closer to Gethin. But when Skye's business with Charles threatens her new friends' livelihood, she has a hard decision to make . . .

ONE SUMMER WEEKEND

Juliet Archer

Alicia Marlowe's life as an executive coach is well under control — until she meets her new client, Jack Smith. Jack's reputation precedes him, and Alicia knows immediately that he spells trouble. Not least because he reminds her of someone else — a man who broke her heart and made her resolve never to lower her guard again. As long as she keeps Jack in his place, Alicia thinks she might just make it through unscathed. But Jack has other ideas — including a 'business' trip to the Lake District . . .